KILLING O'REILLY

The Assassination of America's Most Famous Bloviator

Jane White

ISBN: 1500131105
ISBN 13: 9781500131104

As of the writing of this book Bill O'Reilly was still very much alive. I'm not sure why, though. It does seem that he enrages a great many people and with at least a small militia's worth of gun-toting extremists searching to make their mark in the annals of martyrdom...

So why write a book that depicts a very much alive cause célèbre being shot in the face? It seemed like the right time. O'Reilly will probably live many more years annoying people who still think for themselves yet cannot escape his reach. According to statistics which I just made up O'Reilly will most likely die of coronary disease, alone, but certainly not destitute. Why write an alternative ending for the guy who grew his fortune by rewriting history? I couldn't think of a reason not to.

Read about O'Reilly squaring off against Billy Joel at a high school hockey game, smoking weed and drinking pints in London, and in a Texas discotheque shaking his groove thing. Oh yeah, and he gets shot in the face while doing what he does best, bloviating in front of an audience. It's all in here, and more.

But this isn't just about events that helped to shape Bill O'Reilly. You'll also meet Max Barnes. No matter how bad things got for him he couldn't take his own life but decided to take O'Reilly's instead. His story will move you. Max survived his abusive drunkard parents, being bullied at school, homelessness, and prison only to be driven mad by the bloviating O'Reilly. You will cheer for him and pity him before you wonder if he had it in him to kill O'Reilly. Jeannie Redmont was O'Reilly's number one fan. As a teen she was a Goldwater Girl with aspirations to serve in public office. One false move in high school though and she found herself pregnant and married living the life of a different kind of servitude. And then there is Jill Brown, my favorite character. She joined the force to honor her fallen father. She wore her badge with pride and distinction, but at what cost? Her personal life and her job were pulling her in opposite directions and when Bill O'Reilly was shot on her watch she came to realize some hard truths.

So enjoy this story that is much more than just a giant windbag getting gassed. And the next time you stand on your soapbox and run your mouth because you think this is 'Murica and you have the right to say whatever the hell you want without suffering the consequences know that there is always someone crazier than you who thinks you don't.

Jane White

PROLOGUE

9 AUGUST 2014

The man with less than four days to live sat in a modest lounge chair on a dimly lit stage, squaring off against an audience member. Bill was on his Boldest and Freshest Tour of 2014. Dennis Miller was there. They were in the small, conservative city of Jackson, Michigan.

The middle-aged woman in the front row was remonstrating O'Reilly over his views on gun registration as a means to an end in reducing gun violence. Her hands trembled as she went on to say the tactic was unlikely to have a noticeable effect on gun violence. Her voice cracked as she compared it to tossing a pebble into a stormy ocean. "The tiny ripples would be devoured by the massive waves," she said.

The woman continued. "We need to get rid of the guns; we don't need them anymore. Making more laws that won't be enforced will not solve our problem!"

Bill was stoic as he said, "Ma'am, listen, I've had forty-five years of experience with this issue. I've seen gun violence firsthand. First, it is un-American, even anti-American, to suggest that we throw the United States Constitution out the window. It's ludicrous, and it won't happen. Second, I've met the thugs and criminals who perpetrate gun crimes. I've met with the lawmakers and law enforcers. I know what I'm talking about here."

The woman interrupted and said, "Sir, I have first-hand experience with this issue, too. My son committed suicide with a registered gun."

Several women in the audience gasped audibly and covered their mouths. The mourning mother recited statistics regarding gun-related deaths in an attempt to sway O'Reilly.

In nearly four decades of journalism, sixty-four-year-old Bill O'Reilly had seen it all. He had heard this argument too. He hushed the audience, then stood and walked to the edge of the stage. He was calm as he began his rebuttal.

"Ma'am, I am sorry your son took his own life, truly. No parent should ever have to live through such a tragedy, but—and I know this isn't a popular opinion—but if you had been aware of your son's condition, and you had been doing your job as a caring parent by, say, maybe locking the guns in a childproof safe or talking to your son about depression, chances are he would be alive today, yes?"

The woman began sobbing. An older woman seated next to her reached out to her, but the crying woman pushed her hand away in frustration.

A few men seated immediately around her fidgeted in their seats as they looked around, suddenly afflicted by a guilty conscience. The older woman whose consoling hand had been rebuffed wiped silent tears from her eyes.

The dejected mother's leg began shaking as Bill continued speaking directly to her.

Bill gently proceeded to defend his position on the federal registration he claimed would solve the gun violence issue by allowing cops to do their job.

The woman was suddenly furious and yelled, "No! You are not listening to me! My son committed suicide with a *registered* gun. Don't you get that? We need to get rid of all of the guns!"

The theater fell silent for a moment.

"As I said, I'm sorry about what your son did, but *you,* ma'am, are not listening to *me.*"

Bill opined that a federal registration, bolstered by a mandatory minimum sentence for violators, would be a useful tool for cops when stopping and searching gangbangers, street thugs, and other degenerates and criminals on the street who carried illegal weapons. He claimed the cops could then haul them away and a judge could put them away for a minimum of ten years' hard labor, thereby preventing them from committing another act of gun violence. Bill told her he was certain that once word got out that there was a federal mandatory minimum of ten years' hard labor for gun charges, gun violence would come to a screeching halt.

The haggard woman, her chest rising and falling with deep breaths, countered that her son had been neither a gang member nor a thug. That he had no criminal record at all. That he never left the house with the gun. That he seemed okay right up until the day he put the pistol in his mouth and squeezed the trigger.

Many members of the audience were leaning mouth to ear with frenetic whispering.

For a moment Bill looked as though he would relent and cede the point to the anguished mother. He didn't. Rather, he paused for a moment then insisted that his idea would work in dealing with bad guys but that he understood the issue of mental health as a separate but equally important one. An issue he hoped would be addressed by this President, and soon.

Then O'Reilly skillfully ran down a litany of statistics and facts as he knew them regarding gun violence with the confidence of Senator Obama debating Senator McCain. The woman ceded to O'Reilly with a dismissive wave of her hand. Her head hung low, wiping tears from her cheeks, she retook her seat.

The audience, unsure how to respond, applauded, some more enthusiastically than others. Bill hushed the worked-up crowd as he retook his seat and continued with his show. Seated to his left in an identical chair, Bill's longtime show partner and coconspirator, Dennis Miller, was smiling.

Normally Dennis thoroughly enjoyed watching Bill use his vast vocabulary and vault of facts to verbally beat down hecklers. There seemed to be at least one in every town, someone who bought a ticket just for a chance to confront Bill in a public arena. Bill was always prepared for those confrontations. But this time Dennis was smiling because he was hiding something. He tended to smile when he felt ashamed. He knew he couldn't just walk over and hug the woman and tell her how touched he was by her story. He wanted to. Sometimes Dennis didn't like his job very much.

As the show continued, the audience relaxed in to a comfortable state of pensive observation. The lights went low; the energy in the room mellowed.

Bill was hitting his stride as he bemoaned several recent press releases from the White House. He was sitting in the lounge chair that traveled with him from show to show across the country. He was leaning back slightly, his legs stretched out, his feet crossed. Bill was in charge. He was joking lightly with Dennis about words and semantics and how he would never want the job as the White House press secretary because he would never be able to keep a straight face when he was given the day's script to read for the press. The crowd laughed on cue.

Dennis was laughing as he tried to blurt out his prepared supporting rant on the subject when Bill glanced slightly to his right as a shot rang out from the shadows.

Dennis rocked backward. Bill was knocked off his chair. He landed between his chair and Dennis's.

=

Max Barnes had arrived at the theater an hour before the show began. He was surprised at the number of people already there. Thankfully, most of them were gathered in the lobby and near the concession stand, drinking beer and wine.

He'd wanted to get to the theater early so he could be sure to snag a good seat for carrying out his mission.

Max skipped the concessions, walked down the gently sloping main aisle, and found the perfect seat for the job.

The house lights were on in the theater. There were people scattered here and there on the main seating level. Max could hear a few conversations coming from the balcony seats.

Nobody seemed to notice Max in his seat. He slouched a little lower, trying to be as inconspicuous as possible. For more than thirty minutes he stared straight ahead. He was looking at the stage but not focusing on a thing.

Another fifteen minutes passed, and Max heard some feet shuffling and hushed conversation coming from backstage. He saw a head poke out from around the massive stage curtain and scan the now rapidly filling theater. A second head poked out from behind the curtain and also scanned the crowd.

Five more minutes passed. A young man emerged from behind the curtain and walked to center stage. He thanked the crowd for making it a sold-out show. Applause erupted as if he had just announced that everyone would be sharing in Bill's massive profits from ticket sales. He told the crowd that Bill and Dennis would be coming out in just a moment. More applause. He asked everyone to please be respectful of Bill and Dennis and not to interrupt the show. He reminded the audience of the swag for sale in the main lobby and said he was proud to announce Bill's new book, *Killing Hitler*. He thanked everyone for coming and then introduced Bill and Dennis. Standing ovations all around. The lights went dim.

Max was sitting left of center in the fifteenth row of the floor section. The slight incline of the theater seating put him nearly at eye level with Bill. He was fingering the deep scar that ran across his chin, a habit he'd had for thirty-five years. Fifty-nine-year-old Max Barnes was restless and uncomfortable watching Bill and Dennis. Max imagined Bill O'Reilly as a modern-day Jim Jones grooming his minions. He looked side to side for any genuflecting followers.

The applause from the audience for Bill's verbal victory over a distraught mother caused his stomach to knot. Max did not understand how seemingly normal people could cheer for the death of a troubled young man. Max had experienced plenty of reasons for suicide. He felt sorry for the mother. He felt regret for the dead boy.

Tucked into the waistband of his jeans was a .22 caliber semiautomatic, a Ruger SR22 Rimfire pistol fitted with a silencer. The compact, lightweight weapon was easily concealed under Max's gray hooded sweatshirt. Max put his hand on the pistol's grip through the heavy sweatshirt.

His seat was cloaked in shadow, but he could see Bill clearly under the dim stage lighting. Max didn't know whether he could go through with his plans. He wasn't committed. He thought about just standing up and walking out in the middle of the show. But drawing attention to himself was not a good idea. He sat. And fidgeted, and began to sweat. He wished he had worn something other than a sweatshirt. But he knew that in Central Michigan a man out for an evening would draw no extra attention just because he wore a sweatshirt in August. Several others in the audience were also wearing hooded sweatshirts. Max touched the gun again.

Bill never looked Max's way as he spoke to the capacity crowd. It seemed to him that Bill was looking out just over their heads. Max wanted Bill to look his way at least once before he made his move. He wanted to be acknowledged, if only with a glance.

Max adjusted the weapon. He wished he'd bought a bag of popcorn to distract himself while he waited for just the right time to act. He was afraid somehow that eating popcorn in a crowded theater with a few hundred other people, most of whom were eating popcorn or another theater-appropriate finger food, would draw unnecessary and unwanted attention to himself. He wished he had at least bought a fountain pop to soothe his cotton mouth.

Max scanned the crowd looking for security guards or cops. He didn't see either, then wondered if he was being paranoid. He touched the gun again. He wondered how the people around him would react to seeing Bill being shot in front of them. He wondered what Dennis would do in an emergency. Beads of sweat were forming on his brow.

Max wanted to know what he would do. He wanted to feel the complete surge of power as he pulled the trigger. He wanted to know how he would act when he actually pulled the trigger and saw Bill dead on the floor.

Shocked by the sound of the gunshot, Max watched intently as Bill O'Reilly was rocked out of his lounge chair and hit the floor next to Dennis. The crowd went silent for an instant, and then all hell broke loose.

PART ONE

1

1 NOVEMBER 1966

Bill O'Reilly attended Chaminade High School in Levittown, New York. Chaminade was a private Catholic school for boys. O'Reilly participated in several extracurricular activities, including the debate team. He thrived in all of them.

Seventeen-year-old O'Reilly was preparing for a debate against his classmate Barry Bousche. The subject of the debate was gun control—its moral validity—and the real and perceived effects it might have on reducing gun violence.

Bill was studying the 1960 Kennedy–Nixon debates, the first presidential debates to be televised. Bill had transcripts of the debates, several news articles about them, and a handful of photographs.

Young Bill knew that studying Nixon's defeat was his key to winning. It was Nixon's posture and appearance that Bill studied. He was fascinated by the visual cues that had been perceived as detrimental by journalists and the public: the sweating and constant wiping of his face with a handkerchief, the pale and sickly appearance, the relatively aged look next to JFK.

Nixon had been a relentless campaigner and refused to waste time sitting idly by during the day of the first televised debate. He ignored his advisors and campaigned throughout the day at a rigorous pace. Not fully recovered from a recent hospital visit, Nixon appeared to most around him to be pale and worse for the wear. What he believed to be a show of strength and perseverance would prove to be a show of weakness and foolish pride.

At the television station, Nixon's handlers and the television producers advised him to wear makeup for the camera. They explained how the camera created shadows and could distort his appearance. Nixon, in a misguided sense of machismo, refused to wear the makeup. He did not understand television, camera angles, and lighting. He was a politician.

Kennedy, on the other hand, had embraced the idea of wearing makeup for the camera. He had also taken the advice of his advisors and relaxed his campaign schedule before the debate. As a result, he appeared youthful and energetic.

The young Bill O'Reilly was a history buff and consummate learner. He understood the invaluable lessons that lay in defeat. The important lesson he learned from the first televised debate between Kennedy and Nixon was about perception and how to gain strength from it rather than falling victim to it.

The debate at Chaminade wasn't going to be televised, of course. Bill wouldn't be wearing makeup. His looks and his general appearance were not a problem; he knew he was handsome. He was thinking about another aspect of how perception could win or lose votes. Bill was looking to use his size and his powerful speaking voice to gain an advantage over his smaller, weaker opponent.

Bill was popular by every measure in high school. One reason his peers liked him was his generosity and unselfishness. He was always available to help his friends when they called upon him. So, naturally, if Bill asked a favor, his friends eagerly responded.

A particular friend of his, Joe Laughlin, worked on the stage crew. Bill knew that in order to fully exploit his size advantage over his opponent, he needed to have the lecterns nearly side by side. So he went to Joe and asked him to move the lecterns next to each other rather than having them at either end of the stage. Joe lived two doors down from Bill, and the boys had been friends all the way back to a time before either even knew how to ride a bicycle. Joe trusted Bill and did not question his motives. Bill wanted the audience to see Barry Bousche looking up to him, to drink in his physical prowess. He did not want them thinking too much about what he was saying.

Bill also considered the long-term benefit of the move in terms of how his peers would view him after the debate. While he was already popular, with a commanding win he believed they would see him as stronger and smarter, too. That his ability to persuade them would multiply. He was correct, of course.

Before the auditorium began filling up, while Barry looked on from stage left, Bill practiced behind the lectern. He practiced where he would hold his hands and how to position his arms relative to his body. He practiced emphasizing certain verbal cues using his hands and fingers. He practiced prosody. Bill believed that his vocal control, his rhythm, would indicate confidence in his words.

Nobody ever accused Bill of having a weak vocabulary; he studied his dictionary like his Bible. He had a rigid schedule of learning ten new words a day. Bill was cautious, though, not to be condescending to his audience, only peppering his speech with a few new words. He knew that speakers who were confident in what they were saying were more likely to be trusted. At well over 6 feet tall and 170 pounds, Bill imagined having a commanding presence behind the lectern, towering over his opponent, Barry Bousche, who came in nearly a foot shorter and 20 pounds lighter. Preparedness was everything to Bill O'Reilly.

Bill watched from backstage as students and teachers began filling seats. His confidence didn't quell his anxiousness. His heart was pounding, his palms were sweating. He was minutes away from being in the spotlight.

When the two students walked out on stage and took their places side by side behind their lecterns, the effect was immediate and clear. Barry Bousche, normally confident and well prepared, was unnerved standing next to the towering O'Reilly.

Bill's powerful voice boomed out over the full auditorium with confidence; he'd learned how to project his voice as a choir boy. Barry's voice barely carried to the back rows; he spoke as if he were conversing at the dinner table. Bill was a commanding orator already and knew how to play to the audience. Barry was intimidated by Bill and struggled throughout the debate.

Bill won the debate handily that day. When it was over, he went to his opponent and shook his hand. He congratulated him on a solid effort and wished him better luck next time. Bill was nothing if not gracious.

=

Some 670 miles away, at Parkside Middle School in Jackson, Michigan, twelve-year-old Max Barnes was confronting his fears. The bully sitting on his chest was thirteen-year-old Freddy Green, and Freddy hadn't missed many meals growing up. Freddy weighed in at nearly double Max's weight and had a full three inches of height on him.

Freddy was a known schoolyard bully who had been held back the previous year, putting him in Max's class. Freddy didn't really like anybody, but he especially despised Max. Max never knew the reason Freddy disliked him so. Maybe there wasn't one.

Max was the runt of the class, timid and wholly misunderstood. He had been picked on since the first grade. In the beginning, it was mostly just being laughed at or left out of games on the playground. Names did too hurt, Max knew. But kicks and punches hurt more. And every year it got worse.

Now in the boys' bathroom, Freddy had Max on the urine-stained floor, his knees pinning Max's shoulders down hard. Freddy was trying to make Max cry by torturing him in front of a small group of peers. He was alternately punching Max in the face and in the crotch. Blood smeared Max's face, and he felt dizzy from the repeated blows to his privates. But he would not give in and cry for Freddy's entertainment. He refused to do that. Crying was a sign of weakness. His father had taught him that.

The stark cruelty of the act was normal for Max Barnes. His life was one act of violence after another. Max had been a favorite target of violent schoolyard bullies since the first time he got pushed down during recess and refused to tattle on the bully. Regardless of the type of abuse perpetrated against him, the goal was the same: to make Max Barnes cry. Over the years it had become some kind of twisted game for each new bully to try to succeed where the others failed.

He was the regular recipient of wedgies and swirlies. Once, Max was waiting in the lunch line when a bully stabbed him in the leg with a #2 pencil. Another time, as he was walking up a flight of stairs, a bully had grabbed him by the hair from behind and pulled Max down the stairs.

Too often the only attention Max got at school was negative, even from the teachers. Somehow his being bullied by his peers translated to being singled out by his teachers. He tended to be punished automatically for infractions he had not committed. If a teacher was hit by a spitball, Max found himself getting paddled in front of the class. If students erupted in spontaneous laughter, Max found himself being paddled in front of the class. If any other student in his class was scolded for any other infraction and pointed the finger at Max, he found himself being paddled in front of the class.

By the time Max found himself on the floor of the bathroom with Fat Freddy Green squeezing the air out of his lungs as he punched him in the balls, he was a clinically depressed outcast who was liked by no one, and hated everyone.

With four of his peers standing idly by as he was tortured by someone twice his size for nothing more than existing, Max felt anger building deep inside him. Freddy laughed as he leaned back slightly and twisted just enough to deliver another blow to Max's bruised privates. He was getting careless as the torture session drew on. Max sensed an opportunity to finally fight back when he felt Freddy's weight shift. With every ounce of strength he could muster, he toppled Freddy.

Max jumped to his feet. Freddy was on his back, scrambling to get to his feet. Before he could get his bearings, Max kicked him in the crotch. Freddy cried out in pain as he dropped his hands to guard against another low blow. Max seized the opportunity to stomp him right in the teeth. The first blow to Freddy's face was devastating. Freddy's head ricocheted off the concrete floor with a sickening thud. The second blow shattered teeth. Blood running from his mouth pooled with the blood running from the back of his head.

Max had knocked out several teeth with the third blow. The four boys who had been laughing a moment ago scrambled for the exit.

Before Max could regain his composure, several teachers burst onto the bloody scene. They were stopped in their tracks by the violent scene. Max was huddled against the wall between two urinals. He was staring wide-eyed at Freddy, his knees tucked to his chest. Freddy was sobbing, spitting blood through his mangled mouth. When the principal burst in behind them, the teachers snapped back to attention. Two of them dropped to their knees beside Freddy. The principal went for Max. One teacher ran back to the office and called the police and the paramedics.

Freddy was rushed to the hospital. His injuries were severe. His posse told the principal it had all been Max's fault. They told the police that Max had attacked Freddy for no reason. Max thought about pulling his pants down and showing them his bruised privates. But with no one to corroborate his version of the story, Max knew there was no point.

The principal had tried to call Max's parents but was unable to reach them. Max was remanded to the Jackson City Police. He was scared. The arresting officers cuffed him and put him in the back of the squad car.

Driving away from the school, Max looked out the back window and saw the crowd of students and teachers watching him being carted off to jail. He sat still, not crying or whining or complaining. What was the point? He knew they all believed he was guilty. Nobody would believe he was just defending himself against a bully.

At the city jail, police officers made several attempts to reach Max's parents. Because Max was only twelve, the police couldn't put him in an adult jail cell. Instead, they cuffed him to a handrail in the sally port while they continued their attempt to reach his parents.

The sally port smelled of gas and oil, and Max could hear constant clanging of metal coming from inside the jail. He was scared. He was shivering in his well-worn short-sleeved shirt. And hungry. And worse than all that, he had to move his bowels.

Max was afraid. One of the cops had told him that what he'd done would earn him a good bit of time in juvenile hall. The cop said that tough guys like Max who think it is OK to bloody a guy up at school learn to be good boys or they end up graduating to prison. Max wanted to tell him that he wasn't a tough guy, that he had only been standing up to a bully. Max didn't want to end up in juvenile hall, and he certainly did not want to graduate to prison.

The police finally reached his parents early that evening. They refused to come to the jail even after the officer told them how serious the charge was. In their warped minds, they believed that if the cops had him then he must be guilty. Max wasn't really surprised his parents refused to come get him from jail, but that didn't make him feel any better about it.

The same cop who'd told Max how much trouble he was in also told him about his parents not coming for him. The cop didn't seem too surprised either. He told Max that because of his age the police were not permitted to detain him overnight in the adult jail. He said they had to turn him over to the juvenile authorities. The cop left Max sitting alone in the sally port until the juvenile authorities showed up for him.

2

14 JANUARY 1967

O'Reilly and some of his hockey teammates were huddled behind the stands near center ice. The Chaminade Flyers were set to challenge the Ionia Prep Gaels. Bill and his teammates were reviewing some new plays and the Gaels' statistics from the previous season. They were looking for any statistical weaknesses to exploit.

Bill said, "Listen, guys, we need to be prepared for whatever they're going to throw at us tonight. We can do this as a team."

Mark Coghlan, the team's forward, offered, "Hey, Billy, I have some information I think might help us out."

"Oh yeah?" Bill said with one eyebrow cocked.

"Well, I heard that the Gaels' forward might have injured a wrist while working. He's going to have a heck of a time driving any hard shots at the net."

Brian Hanegan, the teams' left-side defenseman, threw in his two cents. "It might help us steal too. If he's hurt, he won't be able to defend either."

Bill said, "Wait a minute now. We don't know if he's really injured. Mark, who told you this?"

"Well . . ." Mark hesitated as he looked down at his shoes.

"Mark, what say you?" Bill asked, stepping to face Mark.

"Hear me out, fellas. Remember that girl I met at the soda shop last week? Well, we went out for a slice and got to talkin' about the game. She said she really liked hockey guys. Said her friend happened to know the Gaels' forward and knew he had hurt himself at work. Said she was real happy to help us out."

Bill said, "Something doesn't smell right about this whole thing. What makes you think we can trust her?"

Mark replied, "Well, see now, I got to third base with her, so that must count for somethin'." He started laughing.

The gang all laughed and began pushing Mark around like a pinball, mocking him by making kissing sounds into the crooks of their arms and cooing to each other. After a few moments of the lighthearted jostling, Bill brought them back around to the problem of the validity of the information. He wanted to know the facts and only the facts. He had told his teammates that without being able to verify the injury, they were to play as if they hadn't heard the rumor at all.

As the gang continued to review the new plays, a group of boys entered the arena in a tight huddle. Bill recognized these guys from another school. They were all dressed in denim jackets and blue jeans, with long slicked-back hair and single cigarettes tucked behind their ears. They were wearing black leather work boots rather than the fashionable sneakers of the Chaminade boys.

The group of jocks recognized the burnouts from Hicksville High and stopped talking to watch their moves. Bill suspected the shortest guy in the group of burnouts to be the leader. Bill knew his reputation. He hung out in piano bars and smoked pot and drank beer. He was a thug. Bill knew they were the same age because they had crossed paths a couple of times over the years at other school-related events. While economically the two groups were in the same category of working-class heroes, socially they were worlds apart and their social statuses were a barrier that would become an impenetrable wall.

The diminutive burnout with long hair and bushy burnsides was playing it cool in the middle of his group. They had stopped only a few feet away from Bill and his gang, near center ice. One of the burnouts removed the cigarette from behind his ear and struck a match to light it.

O'Reilly was aghast the visiting thug would so blatantly disregard Chaminade's no-smoking policy and shouted "Hey!" at the boy before he could light the cancer stick.

The group of thugs looked at Bill. The jocks quickly looked at Bill and then at the boy with the cigarette and his gang. All of them were silent; none of them moved a muscle as they all locked in a stare-down.

It was an all-too-common sight: the preppy Catholic school boys facing off against the burnouts from

Hicksville. The one holding the cigarette extinguished his match and threw it on the arena floor. Bill had little tolerance for the thugs and their foul language and long hair. He couldn't understand why they chose to be thugs and acted the way they did.

A few moments of tense silence passed between the young men before it was broken by a third group's joining the party, a group of girls in high heels and higher hair wearing bright red lipstick and blowing bubblegum bubbles and popping them while making lewd gestures with their tongues.

The girls stopped and looked from the group of burnouts to the group of jocks and back to the burnouts. Some of the jocks were staring at some of the girls, and the teammate with the inside edition on the Gaels' forward was making eye contact with the only blonde in the group. Bill slapped him on the shoulder and pointed at the girl and asked him if she was his source. With a sheepish shrug and a nod, he admitted she was in fact his informant. Bill's face flushed red as the girls walked toward the other boys and began laughing and talking with them.

Bill knew then that the information was bogus, and he was furious with his mate for falling for such an obvious ploy.

The blonde the teammate had been rooked by locked arms with the leader of the burnout pack as he made eye contact with O'Reilly. The thug smiled before turning on his heel and laughed as he walked away. The jocks returned to studying the plays as the girls and their guys walked off to take their seats in the stands.

═══

Max stood in the chow line, eyeing the kid responsible for scooping the slop onto the trays. Max thought the kid was bad and deserved to be in juvenile hall. Max took a step closer as the line moved forward. The food smelled horrible. Max didn't know what it was; it looked like macaroni with some kind of ground meat in heavy brown gravy. Everything was always covered in some gravy or sauce. One more step; the kid shoved his ladle into the deep pan and looked up at Max. Max just stood and watched. The kid smiled wide at Max as he hawked a loogie into the ladle of slop before dumping it on Max's tray. Max looked away quickly. His stomach was growling in protest of the hunger pangs; his nostrils flared in protest of the stench.

At the end of the serving line, another kid who Max thought probably deserved to be in juvenile hall tossed two pieces of white bread onto his tray. Max just looked intently at the floor and turned away. He knew glaring at them or confronting them would only lead to trouble. And Max was already dealing with enough trouble.

Max went to the table reserved for losers and took his seat. He was hungry; he had been hungry every day in juvenile hall. Most days went just the same way, with Max getting a little extra on top. Sometimes it was spit; sometimes the kid would dig a huge booger from his nose and plunk it down. The worst times were the ones they didn't do anything in front of Max but laughed so hard he was sure they had done something really bad. Sometimes on those days Max would carefully inspect every morsel before eating any of it. Other days he just dug right in while they watched as if it didn't matter what they did. If he didn't want to starve to death, he had to eat something.

He always started by trying to eat around whatever extra toppings they gave him, but sometimes he was so hungry he just ate it all anyway. On the rare occasion the food was actually tolerable, one of the bullies would liberate it from Max, so he didn't have a lot of options.

With his food gone and his stomach queasy, Max returned his tray and headed back to his bunk. The boys were given two hours after supper to play cards or socialize within the unit. Max didn't play cards and he didn't want any more socialization than he already had. He just wanted to press his bunk until lights out so he could get the night's torture over with.

It had all started on his first night there. He had been scared and depressed. He felt completely alone in the world. He had no one to confide in or talk to. At supper that first night, two older boys approached him. They each gave him a chocolate bar and told him not to worry about thanking them. They had left him at the table confused, unsure whether he should eat the chocolate. His stomach had made the call for him. He quickly ate both chocolate bars, taking huge bites and swallowing hard. All the while the boys watched him, smiling and whispering to each other.

After lights out that night, the boys paid Max a visit. One held his arms down as the other pelted him with a sock that had a bar of soap in it. One of the boys leaned in close to Max's ear and whispered, "We own you now." After they sufficiently beat Max, they took turns raping him. Max had never felt such humiliation or pain.

Since that first rape, those two boys had been paying Max fairly regular visits after lights out. In the beginning Max had struggled and tried to fight back. But that only made them more violent. So he did what his survival instincts told him to do—he submitted. It had made his life a little easier. When the boys came, Max closed his eyes and imagined he was somewhere else.

Max was tired. His stomach had ached from one thing or another every day. He began trembling as the boys in the hall started falling asleep. He knew it was almost time to pay his dues. He closed his eyes and wished he were somewhere else. It didn't work, though. He opened his eyes just as the boys descended on him, full of violent lust. He was right where he had always been, in hell.

3

9 OCTOBER 1967

Bill was not like most of his peers. He was more of a casual observer than a participant. He was able to pick up cues from watching others interact. He observed how certain students with affluent or influential parents talked to their professors and school administrators. He observed the students working their way through college in the library or cafeteria, how they treated their peers with admiration, respect, or sometimes jealousy or spite. To him, sometimes watching the action was more exciting than participating. Having watched and learned about a particular subject, he was then able to use his powers of observation to expand his knowledge base.

Sometimes it frustrated Bill that his friends' view of the world was so narrow, that they couldn't see themselves beyond their immediate situation.

"Listen to what I'm telling you, Joe, those Vassar girls are not into us. They don't care about blue-collar guys from the old neighborhood. Come on, man, wise up." Joe Laughlin, one of Bill's oldest childhood friends, had followed Bill to Marist.

"Be smart now, Billy, a college degree and good-payin' job would make any girl happy."

"Nope. No way, Joe. They don't care about a Marist degree. I'm telling you, I've seen the way they look at those Cornell guys. They get all doe-eyed and start twirling their hair and giggling. It's embarrassing, Joe. Listen, I swear I saw one of those Vassar girls drooling over a Princeton guy last weekend. The guy had to proffer his handkerchief, for crying out loud. I'm not kidding here, Joe, drooling."

"You're puttin' me on now, Billy. They're nice girls. We should just go to the dance Saturday night and see what gives, huh?"

"No way. Not after last weekend. I'm not a sidelines kinda guy, Joe. You know that. Besides, I've got plenty of work to do right here on campus. I've got three papers due just this week. I'm not wasting my time chasing girls who don't care to even know I exist. It doesn't make any sense."

Joe turned his back on Bill and walked away, his eyes on the ground, his shoulders sagging. Bill stood his ground. There would be no more chasing Vassar girls.

Bill wanted to concentrate on his studies. He wasn't up for playing games. If he was going to break out of his blue-collar roots and build a path to a higher social standing, he needed to knuckle down and get refocused. He knew there would be more times when he would have to forgo chasing girls in order to graduate with top honors and continue his education. Bill knew that education was his ticket to a higher standard of living and a better quality of life. There would be plenty of time for girls later.

Bill watched Joe cross the courtyard and disappear into the library. He liked Joe. Joe was smart, hardworking, and a loyal friend. Bill decided he would call Joe later to invite him over to play cards. He stood for another moment or two, then turned and began walking to the dining hall.

As Bill reached for the dining hall door, he heard, "Hi, Billy, want to share a table?" Linda Rustenburg had sneaked up behind him and caught him off guard.

"Hello, Linda." Bill was smiling. He had seen Linda around campus in the evening. She had been one of the first women to enroll in the night courses at the previously all-male school. "Sure, that would be great." Bill wouldn't admit it to Joe, but he had a crush on Linda.

She was smart and witty with a sense of humor. She also had a va-va-voom quality that drove Bill wild. Something happened to him when he saw her that made him forget whatever else he had been thinking about.

Bill stepped back and held the door for Linda. Her sweater was stretched tight across her ample chest. He watched her cross the threshold and shook his head as he exhaled slowly and quietly.

Girls had a way about them that sometimes rendered men unable to resist temptation. Bill knew he didn't have time to chase Linda, even as easy as she was making it to catch her. He knew a brief affair with her would lead to nowhere good.

"What's on the menu today, Billy?" Linda had the type of sultry voice that made the most innocent words sound provocative.

"I'm not sure. I was going to get a sandwich before my next class." Bill didn't want to lead Linda on. He didn't play games with girls. That kind of thing never ended well for either party.

"That sounds good to me. I'm heading to the library after a quick bite to do research for a paper. Let's grab a table, and you can tell me all about your next class."

Bill and Linda picked up their trays and headed for a quiet table in the corner.

"How are you doing with your evening classes?" Bill asked before chomping into his pastrami sandwich.

"Things are really going well for me. It's a lot of work, yes, but worth it. Hey, I hear Marist is considering opening full enrollment for women next year. That would be great. If it happens, I will definitely be registering for full-time status," she said, smiling all the way to the corners of her eyes.

"Well, I hope to see you around more during the day, then." Bill had a fleeting image of meeting Linda for lunch on a regular basis as he stifled a smile.

"Terrific! I'm sure by then Ronnie will be here too. I would love for you to meet him."

"Ronnie?" Bill took an even larger bite of the sandwich, hoping she was going to say Ronnie was her brother and not her lover.

"My boyfriend from high school. We just hate being away from each other. You remind me of him, tall and handsome."

Just as quick as Bill thought Linda was flirting with him, she seemed not to be. As they finished their sandwiches, Bill thought that even though he watched life from the outside often and took plenty of notes on what made people tick, he might never figure women out.

=

Max Barnes was being led out of juvenile hall by his mother. She was a step ahead of him, going through the heavy glass and steel door. She didn't bother to hold it for him; he wasn't surprised as he stiff-armed the door and walked through. He walked down the steps of the detention center, looked up at the bright blue sky, and took a deep breath of fresh air.

After spending a year in what amounted to a prison for children, he was ready to get on with his life. He wanted desperately to forget the nightmare of being incarcerated with the violent youths. Nobody acted their age—there were no innocent children in there, inside the dark and dirty halls of the detention center. The misguided anger, foul language, and violence were tantamount to torture. They acted the way they had been taught by the adults that raised them: their abusive parents, their corrupt teachers, and their predatory clergymen.

It had been a year since Max had last seen his mother. She did not look well; she seemed to have aged at least five years. Her eyes were sunken, with dark heavy bags underneath. Her hair was wiry and mostly gray. Her skin was pale gray, clammy.

Max felt pity for the woman, though she had earned her scars. As bad as Max knew he'd had it at home, he imagined his mother had it worse. She was trapped in a ruthless marriage to a psychopath, unable to conjure an escape.

She had of course seen the news reports of the women's rights movement and watched the women burning their brassieres in protest. She had heard the women on the street talking about having a say in their households. She also knew none of that applied to her; in her world she didn't have the rights of a kept dog.

Oppression wasn't a word in her vocabulary; it was a burden she toiled under her entire life, and one she would not escape by burning her underwear or having her voice heard.

Max continued following his mother along the walk toward the parking lot.

"Max, your father can't wait to see you."

Max was a step behind his mother. He could hear the insincerity in her voice. He cocked a disbelieving eye at her. "I'm sure he can't."

"He misses you, is all." His mother was speaking softly, looking at her feet as she took each deliberate step.

"He misses me?" Max was looking at the back of his mother's head, forgetting what her face looked like.

"Yes, Max, don't be so surprised. He hasn't seen you in a long time." Her tone was anything but that of a loving caring mother: cold and distant, nearly mechanical.

"It was his choice. He knew where I was." Max was angrier than he expected and shocked by his own ferocity.

His mother turned so quickly, he was caught completely off guard when she slapped his face. "Listen to me, boy. You don't start sassin' me after a year of being away. No school, no chores, sleepin' all day while I been home takin' care everythin' by myself."

Max stood in place as she spat her angry words, stinging his face like acid. That was his mother, teeth bared, hatred spilling from every pore. When she finished scolding him, she turned and continued walking.

Following his mother along the concrete walk of the detention center, Max felt a shiver run up his spine as he realized things had not changed at home, at least not for the better. Dark scenes from his childhood raced through his mind. He had witnessed too much abuse in his short life. He knew his parents were no good. He also knew what was in store for him when he got home.

It was a twisted vicious circle of abuse that Max had hoped the year in juvenile hall would help diminish. Now, with the events of the first night in juvenile hall firmly imprinted in his memory, Max believed life was going to bc hcll for him cvcrywhcrc hc wcnt. Max kncw he did not want to see what his twisted parents had in store for him when he got home.

At the car, Max hesitated for a moment, debating whether to make a break for it. Before his mother noticed his hesitation, he opened the rusty car door and got in. She slammed her door and automatically lit a cigarette. She was breathing hard after the short walk. Max could see sweat across her brow. She looked at him as if he were some parasitic insect draining her lifeblood. Max rolled his window down and crowded the door to get as far away from her as possible.

The drive to his parents' house would take less than fifteen minutes in light traffic. He was getting sick thinking about stepping into that old house and seeing his father with a bottle of booze in one hand and a belt in the other.

He needed to get out of the car long before then. The first traffic signal was green. His mother drove through the intersection, oblivious to the traffic. She just stared straight ahead, puffing her cigarette. The next one turned red, and his mother brought the car to a stop. Max's heart pounded. He could feel his mother's eyes on him, condemning him. He put his hand on the door handle. His mother looked forward. The light turned green; his mother pushed down the gas pedal. Max pulled the door handle. The car was quickly gaining speed as Max jumped out and rolled on the pavement. He jumped to his feet. Max sprinted in the opposite direction from the way his mother's car was travelling. His mother yelled for him to stop. She was forced by traffic to drive through the intersection before she could pull over. By then, Max was out of sight.

Max knew his mother would pay a dear price for his actions. That was something he would not feel guilty over, though. He had paid dearly for years, and he didn't owe her a thing.

4

23 MAY 1969

Queen Mary College in London provided an opportunity for young O'Reilly to learn about other cultures through life experiences. Bill could have attended any number of colleges in the States and experienced various subcultures of his own, but he thrived on knowing how cultures the world over experienced life. Books and movies provided Bill with only a limited experience of the world, and he wanted to see it, feel it, and touch it.

Throughout his middle and late teens, while Bill grew in physical stature, he also consciously developed personality traits he knew would be beneficial for someone wanting to build meaningful long-term relationships.

At Queen Mary College, O'Reilly towered over most of his peers and drew a lot of positive attention from the female students. With his rugged good looks, charming smile, and affable personality, O'Reilly found it easy to befriend both male and female students.

While Bill talked easily with both genders and was by no means shy, he spent the majority of his time concentrating on his studies. It was his rigid study ethic that helped him excel in all of his course studies. And earning top honors was his top priority. But that didn't mean he was infallible.

Even though he desperately wanted to earn high marks and therefore dedicated most of his energy to his studies, it wasn't always enough to stifle his growing fascination with the opposite sex. A self-proclaimed slow starter with girls, Bill was finally coming into his own with the fairer sex. And after all, part of experiencing another culture is experiencing its women.

Sitting on the east lawn reading *Melbourne* by Lord David Cecil, Bill had been approached by a group of women. Bill could often be found reading a book on campus. On the chillier days he took advantage of the library, but on beautiful spring days such as this one he preferred to be outside in the fresh air. Deep in thought, he had hardly realized they were standing patiently in a semicircle in front of him, waiting to be acknowledged. When one mock-coughed then giggled, he finally looked up and smiled.

Bill was sure he recognized one as a classmate or at least a fellow student, but the others he had not seen on campus at all. He reasoned that just because he had not seen them did not mean that they were not students. It was, after all, a large campus and only part of a larger network of colleges. Besides, Bill wasn't a gawker. He didn't waste much time memorizing the various faces of the female students or taking mental note of the comings and goings of female visitors.

On that warm Friday afternoon, though, Bill was enjoying the attention paid him by the group of women. Always easy with a greeting, Bill said, "Hello." And waited.

The speaker for the group said, "Hello. I'm Anna. My friends and I noticed you sitting here all alone on this beautiful spring day and wanted to know if you would like some company."

Not used to be singled out by large groups of attractive girls, Bill was a little on edge about their bold approach and apparent candor. A naturally suspicious guy, Bill looked askance at the girls. Nonetheless, when Anna got around to inviting Bill to forgo reading his book for a night of pub crawling, he was on board.

Anna introduced the three other girls, Julia, Caroline, and Nat. Nat was a freshman, the other two sophomores, and Anna a junior. Bill smiled at each in turn as she was introduced.

Normally reserved Bill decided to relax and see where the night—and the girls—would take him. He wasn't exactly the guy around town when it came to the fairer sex, and while he was a tremendous opponent on the sports field—whether it be baseball or hockey—in part because of his ability to master the playbook, he didn't exactly have a master game plan for sleeping around.

All were eager to get the party started even though it was still only midday. Bill suggested they first take a walk through the park and maybe pick up some bread, cheese, and wine and talk for a bit before heading to the pub.

Nat squealed in excitement at the idea of spending the day with the handsome American student, and the other girls laughed at her display. Bill smiled and loosened his tie, and they started off.

Along the way Bill talked mostly with Anna while the younger three followed behind, skipping and jumping arm in arm in high spirits. Anna suggested they stop off at the bakery near the park to pick up the ingredients for the picnic, and with a giggle she told Bill that they had a special treat for him once they got there. Nat heard Anna tell Bill about the special treat and shrieked with excitement again, barely able to contain herself. All the girls erupted with laughter, and Bill couldn't stop from blushing.

Bill's spirits were on the rise as his guard began falling. He and Anna talked about classes and schedules and lectures they planned on skipping and professors who tended to be full of air whose lectures ran on and on. In the back of his mind, though, Bill wondered about that special treat. He was inexperienced in such matters and couldn't fathom just what it might be.

Mallory Bakery was a popular spot for the more refined students in search of ciabatta bread, cheese, and wine. They took great pride in providing a well-presented picnic basket stuffed with all of the essentials, including crumpets and scones.

The park was only a few blocks from the bakery, and while Anna and Bill stopped to get the food, the other girls ran ahead.

When Bill and Anna arrived, they found Nat, Julia, and Caroline sitting cross-legged on a red-and-blue-striped blanket chattering away about all sorts of nonsensical things young girls talk about. Bill asked the girls about the blanket, and Julia confessed to living nearby.

Bill placed the picnic basket in the center of the blanket and sat down next to Anna, and the others moved in closer to make a circle.

Nat removed the bottle of wine from the basket as Julia laid out the food. The conversation was light, and the girls giggled at almost everything Bill said or did. Nat poured Bill a glass of wine and winked at him when she handed it to him. *Nat the Nymphet*, he thought, unsure it was an intentional wink. But when Nat tipped her glass to her lips, she winked at him again. The light flirting from Nat surprised Bill, not because he thought he didn't warrant the attention but because he thought that type of attention was better suited for a private encounter.

The afternoon sun was high and warm, with a gentle breeze blowing through the budding spring trees. The five picnickers talked and laughed and flirted until the wine had been drunk, the bread and cheese had been eaten, and the desserts had been devoured.

Anna, Julia, and Caroline all jumped to their feet and ran off, laughing and looking back over their shoulders at Bill and Nat. Bill was a little surprised by the sudden fleeing of the girls but remained seated because Nat the Nymphet did. She smiled at Bill and asked him if he was ready for the surprise she had for him. Bill blushed. He didn't know what to say or do. Nat slipped her hand up her top into her brassiere. Bill thought she was going to remove her brassiere right there in the park, but instead she slowly pulled her hand out to show she was holding a joint. She smiled wide at Bill.

Before Bill could protest, she jumped on his lap and put the joint between his lips. Quick as a magician, she had the flame of a lighter at the tip of it. Bill inhaled and watched the end of the joint glow red as the potent smoke burned his lungs and stung his eyes.

Bill was surprised at his action. He had never smoked grass and hadn't intended to that day. But with the girls, the wine, the sunshine, and Nat the Nymphet so cute and flirtatious—he decided to just roll with it for once.

Nat pulled the joint from Bill's lips and took a drag, and with her lungs full of smoke she kissed Bill hard on the mouth and exhaled. She laughed hard and pushed Bill to his back on the grass. Bill let her take control. They finished smoking the joint and kissed and laughed. Bill was excited as his hands roamed all over his nymphet's body.

Nat sat up and grabbed the bottom of her top and started pulling it up just as the other girls came running to the blanket in a fit of laughter. She quickly dropped her hands, downplaying the whole thing. Bill was flushed, buzzed, and relieved. He wasn't sure where Nat had intended to take things, and even though he had been along for the ride, he was glad for the interruption. What he did with a woman was a private affair not to be shared openly in public. He was not proud of his actions up to that point.

After returning their blanket and basket to Julia's pad, the group walked downtown to the first pub and ordered pints all around.

Bill was nineteen years old, and Anna the same; Bill had no idea, really, how old the others were. The legal drinking age then was eighteen, and most pubs served to those as young as fifteen without question because they made up such a huge portion of their customer base. Only when a minor caused trouble for the owner or barkeep would he be cut off. But everyone at the table had been served without question.

The music was loud, the dancing boisterous. Not normally one to imbibe, Bill's head was spinning from the drink and the pot. While Anna, Julia, and Caroline danced and laughed, Nat came to the table and sat on Bill's lap and kissed him. She was clearly drunk and high. Bill couldn't resist the nubile girl and her advances. He found he was groping her right there at the table, unable to think straight. Nat didn't resist. The more Bill explored her body, the harder she pushed into him.

And just like at the park, Anna and the others broke them up just before things went too far. It was getting late, and Caroline wanted to head to the next pub.

Just a block away, the inebriated group ordered pints all around and before they finished those pints were talking about heading to yet another pub a few blocks away. It was all too much for Bill to keep up with.

At the third pub, again pints were ordered. The girls again danced and laughed. And again Nat returned to the table to make out with Bill, only this time Nat whispered in his ear that she must have him and have him soon, so without saying a thing to the others, the would-be lovers quickly left the pub and headed for Julia's studio apartment.

Bill wished he had protection with him. Even though the pill was widely available, Bill was aware that the greater danger was in sexually transmitted diseases. Bill also knew how babies were made, and unlike many young people, he knew having a child out of wedlock could lead to devastating consequences for the mother and baby, as well as for him. He didn't want whatever was about to happen to cause either of them any residual pain.

After Bill and Nat left the pub, he walked her to Julia's apartment. At the apartment door, Bill kissed his nymphet on the forehead and told her he'd had a splendid time with her but that it was terribly late and he must be going.

Nat said, "Oh Billy, we could have had such a great time." She kissed him once more on the lips, then gently on each cheek, before disappearing into the apartment.

Having no idea what had happened to Nat, Anna went to the police for fear of the worst. The police tracked her down at a local hospital. She had apparently passed out while walking back to the pub to rejoin the other girls and was discovered by an elderly couple who drove her to the hospital to be examined.

She was fine, but the police had many questions for Bill. Bill had many questions for the police, and for the girls, but he held his tongue. It didn't take long for Bill to piece together the puzzle. It turned out that Nat the Nymphet was really Rebecca Greenway, and rather than being a freshman in college, she was a freshman in high school. Nat was visiting Caroline from a neighboring town, and Caroline had thought it would be a harmless prank to introduce her as a freshman from their school. The other girls agreed it was harmless enough, so they all went along with the scheme. Not until they realized that Nat/Rebecca and Bill had left the pub alone did they realize the consequences of their decision. Satisfied with the girls' statements, no charges were filed, and Bill was free to go.

Bill walked back to his dorm in the cool night air, knowing he had narrowly escaped serious criminal charges that would have utterly ruined his future.

=

Behind a small family-owned café called the Early Bird, Max waited for the morning garbage to be hauled out back and tossed in the giant green dumpster. In the beginning he had been shocked at the amount of food left uneaten by the Early Bird diners. But it didn't take long to get over that. It wasn't always easy separating the food from the other garbage, but it was well worth the effort. Max found it ironic that the Early Bird was popular for serving large portions when so much of it ended up in the dumpster. They served their gluttonous portions seven days a week, so Max could at least count on breakfast every day.

Max waited patiently for the day's garbage to be hauled out. Finally the familiar sound of the heavy steel door being unlocked drew Max's attention. The

morning fry cook was carrying two black garbage bags
to the dumpster just a few feet from where Max was
hiding under the delivery ramp of the office next door.

It was always a struggle for Max to count to sixty
before jumping into the dumpster in search of breakfast. Even though Max's stomach growled angrily at its
emptiness, he always counted to sixty just to make sure
the cook wasn't bringing out more garbage.

Just when he thought he wouldn't make it the full
minute, the back door opened again. Max took a deep
breath and waited. It was one of the morning shift wait-
resses taking an early cigarette break. Max's heart sank
as his stomach ached.

Thankfully, she only took a couple of quick puffs
and ran back inside. Max couldn't wait any longer. He
ran and threw himself over the edge of the dumpster
and tore the first bag open. Not much food, mostly
garbage. The second bag was a bit better: a handful
of sausage links, a stack of dry toast, and a pile of
fried potatoes. Just as quickly as he'd jumped into the
dumpster, he jumped out and headed to a safer place
to eat. As he walked he munched on slices of toast to
hold him over. The food pulled at his stomach, and
he wished he had a place to sit down and eat like a
man instead of running to the woods to eat like an
animal.

Along the Grand River were several large wooded
areas that provided shelter from the condemning public eye. Max would never go into the woods at night
because of the high number of homeless men—many
of them considered very dangerous—who camped

there, but during the day he could usually find an area away from the hobos.

Max found a rock to lean against and sat down on the riverbank with his booty. The sausage links coated his lips and mouth with greasy goodness. His stomach ached as he shoved the soggy fried potatoes into his mouth as if they were handfuls of popcorn. With his belly full, he stuffed the rest of the toast in his jacket and lay back on the soft grass.

The term "long summer day" had an entirely new meaning for Max as a homeless person. The hours passed slowly. The mind had plenty of time turn in on itself. Max thought he had a much better understanding of what it meant to be alone, lonely.

However lonely he was, Max knew he would never seek refuge at his parents' house. Being alone was hard to bear, but being beaten and abused was worse.

With the remaining dry toast wrapped in his jacket and his jacket tucked under his arm, the streaks of sunlight warming his body, Max dozed off.

5

10 MARCH 1972

Mr. O'Reilly sat in the teacher's lounge looking out the long row of large windows. The sun shone bright and warmed his face. He was deep in thought, contemplating his career choice, his future, and the changes he needed to make to correct his course.

Growing up, Bill had observed his family, and at college he'd observed his peers, and he had decided he wanted something different. He didn't have a grand plan to be president and he didn't have a wild desire to be über-rich; his tastes were simple, but he didn't want to toil his life away working a dead-end job that would keep him bound to his working-class roots.

While Bill regarded the working class as the backbone of society and respected his parents as part of that segment, he wanted more. He knew there was a larger world to explore. He knew there was opportunity to be had. And he knew there was greater personal freedom that came with rising above the rank-and-file working-class regime.

O'Reilly decided to start climbing the socioeconomic ladder by choosing a white-collar career. He went into teaching because of the admiration and respect he had felt for many of his teachers in high school. His teachers had been great role models. He was impressed not only with their authority but also with the regard many of the students held for them. Teaching was also a noble profession. He knew he would never get rich as a teacher, but the job came with some perks he thought might make up for the pay. The work days were fixed and relatively short, there were plenty of paid holidays, and he would have summers off. That kind of personal freedom was hard to ignore.

After college he accepted a teaching job in what at the time was considered one of the worst slums in South Florida, in Opa-Locka at the ten-year-old Monsignor Pace High School. It was a solid start to a promising career. If the neighborhood wasn't great, at least the weather was.

When he began teaching, he was hopeful, excited to be shaping young minds as his teachers had for him. But Bill knew teaching was more than just learning English or memorizing history; it was about guiding students. Bill understood that students needed not only academic instruction but also moral guidance. He saw how students were engrossed in sex, drugs, and rock-and-roll and knew he could steer them down a righteous path. He immediately took action by having frank and open discussions with his students about moral fortitude, dressing with respect, and practicing proper social etiquette. He understood how critical it was that they also get emotional security and perspective in dealing with social pressures and stereotypes. Those were things he knew didn't come from a textbook or a hundred-year-old lecture. The young Mr. O'Reilly understood the power of *his* words and the *way* he used them. Bill was aware of his influence on the young students walking the halls of Monsignor Pace High School. He had learned from his years of observing his teachers indirectly and inadvertently influencing their students through their own actions.

It didn't take long for Bill to realize he was up against more than an antiquated methodology and outdated textbooks; he was up against miles of bureaucratic red tape, an incompetent figurehead, the school's administration, its inability to understand the real issues, and its arbitrary rules. The old-guard way of indoctrinating students was alive and woefully resilient.

In addition, he was beginning to feel the rut of the working class: the fixed income, the monthly bills, and the sinking feeling of never getting ahead. He started feeling that he would never get to enjoy those holidays and summer vacations with his mediocre pay.

So there he sat, his future confronting him, demanding an answer. He had one more class before he could escape the confines of the school and figure out what he was going to do next.

When the final bell rang and the students rushed the main doors, Bill decided to reward himself with a steak dinner at one of his favorite local eateries, Gary's Steakhouse. Bill didn't splurge on many luxuries, but a decent meal was worth the extra cost, especially after another dreadful day of dealing with the bureaucratic nonsense of being a high school teacher.

Bill decided to walk to dinner, hoping the fresh spring air would clear his head so he could fully weigh his options and future. Gary's was only a few blocks away from the school on 27th Avenue. Even though the neighborhood was brewing with violence and crime, Bill wasn't worried about walking to dinner. He walked along at an energetic pace and began to relax as the sun gently massaged his broad shoulders. He was feeling better in the fresh spring air. Alive and fit.

Traffic was light through the rough-and-tumble neighborhood, and there were few people on the street that afternoon. A couple of small planes passed overhead, preparing to land at the nearby airport. Rounding the corner onto 27th, Bill could smell the succulent flavors of Gary's wafting through the air. His mouth watered. His stomach growled.

A loud car rumbled past Bill. As the noise faded, Bill heard the patter of running feet coming toward him at a full sprint. He spun around in time to see two young boys, probably in their mid-teens, approaching.

One had a snub-nosed revolver in his right hand, his arm extended to Bill's face. The other was holding a switchblade with a black pearl handle, its blade glimmering in the Florida sun. They had been hiding in the thick bushes on the corner across the street.

The boys were dirty and desperate. The one with the gun in Bill's face was quiet, his trigger finger steady. The other one with the switchblade was barking orders at Bill to give him all of his money. His English was fractured at best. Bill didn't recognize his native tongue. The boy's blade-wielding hand was shaking badly. He was either scared or on drugs; Bill presumed it was both.

He had reflexively raised his hands at the sight of the muggers and their weapons, and as the one continued to demand Bill's wallet, he told them to both stay calm and he would give them whatever money he had on him. He only hoped the few dollars he had in his wallet would appease the crooks rather than irritate them and cause them to shoot him or stab him or both.

Bill remained calm, unafraid. Crime in the area was rising. Drugs, gangs, robbery, and assault were part of the culture now. But he was secure in his faith and had resolved long ago that when it was his time, there would be nothing for him to do but accept it. In that moment, though, Bill knew it wasn't his time.

Tentatively, he reached for his wallet in his inside suit-jacket pocket and pulled it out. With both hands he slowly removed the bills, just eighteen dollars, and handed them over to the one with the gun. Bill held his wallet open so the bandits could see he had no more cash to give.

They hesitated for just a moment, perhaps contemplating shooting him for carrying such a paltry sum of cash, before a car rounded the corner and they made a break for it back toward the bushes across the street. In a flash, they were gone.

Bill just stood and watched them disappear. The car drove by him, none the wiser that he had just been robbed at gunpoint.

He shook his head in disgust. He was angry that he had been so easily robbed in broad daylight only blocks from the school where he was employed as a teacher. He was angry that his muggers were probably illegal immigrants. He was angry he would not be dining at Gary's.

Being robbed was the final push Bill needed to leave Opa-Locka and teaching. He realized he was still standing in the spot where he had been robbed. For another minute he contemplated his future.

He was going to be smarter and work harder at succeeding, at climbing the social ladder. He realized his life had been defined for him by a class system that discouraged most people from ascending the social ladder regardless of their hard work and effort. Bill finally turned around and started his walk back to the school parking lot where he had left his car parked in favor of a leisurely walk in the famous Florida sunshine. Bill wasn't a fatalist, but on that afternoon he wasn't sure it wasn't fate slapping him in the face.

Not only did Bill decide then that he would return to school, he decided he was definitely going into journalism. He knew his voice would be heard. He knew there were things wrong in the world that he would dedicate the rest of his life to righting.

=

Max was on his way to a pawnshop downtown to unload the booty he'd stolen from a purse that morning. He had done it a hundred times. He had a routine. He crossed the street, rounded the corner, and headed for the alley. Max always used the alley entrance to the pawnshop. It drew less attention. As he turned into the alley, he got a weird feeling in his gut. Something wasn't right. He stopped and looked around. He spotted a known heroin junkie hiding behind a dumpster in the alley. Max had seen the junkie around town. He knew the junkie might rob him. Max couldn't wait around for the junkie to leave, though, and continued on with his business.

Max was always straight to the point when getting rid of hot goods, not wanting to draw any unnecessary attention his way. The crooked owner of the pawnshop appreciated it that way, too.

The pawnshop owner was ruthless when he was buying hot product. He paid only pennies on the dollar, knowing the seller usually had no other options.

The stolen purse Max had snatched that day didn't contain much of value. The one item it did have, though, was a diamond ring. One of the three stones was missing from its setting. Max didn't have any idea what the ring's actual value was, hot or not. He knew that the owner wanted it, though, because he offered Max ten dollars for it. That was more than Max ever got in one haul.

With cash in his pocket, Max turned around and headed out of the back door into the alley. He was so elated at his good fortune that he had forgotten about the junkie. Just as the pawnshop door slammed shut, the junkie jumped out from behind the dumpster and with a trembling trigger finger jammed a pistol in Max's face and demanded the money.

Up until that day, Max had been fairly successful at avoiding any confrontations or violence. He wouldn't be able to talk his way out of this one, though. Max had not had any cash in too long; he needed a few things from the store that he couldn't steal and wanted a decent meal, a hot meal that he didn't have to dig out of a garbage can. He wasn't going to be handing over any cash.

The junkie had sunken eyes with dark rings around them. His skin was blotchy, with lesions and contusions on his arms. His teeth rotten and his nose running, he was fidgeting wildly. Max knew that if the gun was loaded, the junkie would just as soon shoot him as he would rob him.

With one quick move, Max dropped to his knees and punched the junkie in the stomach as hard he could. As Max dropped and swung, the junkie pulled the trigger and fired one round just over Max's head, where it ricocheted off the pawnshop wall. The thunder from the gun temporarily deafened Max.

His ears ringing, Max jumped to his feet and wrapped his arms around the junkie, tackling him to the ground and driving his full weight on top of him. The junkie's head made a sickening thud on the concrete, and blood splattered through his greasy hair.

Max jumped to his feet and looked around the alley for any witnesses, then looked down at the limp and lifeless body. For a split second Max thought about grabbing the gun and running, but before he could muster the strength to kneel down and remove it from the dead attacker's hand, he heard a bloodcurdling scream from behind him.

A woman had rounded the corner to the alley, seen Max standing over the dead body, and screamed for all she was worth. Max panicked, and for what felt like an eternity he froze in that spot. He stood unable to even lift a foot. The woman's frantic screams drew the attention of a construction crew driving by, and they too saw Max standing over the lifeless body.

Not until the truck slammed on its brakes and four men jumped from it and began running at Max did he realize that if he didn't run now, he would be in a lot of trouble. Blinking, he broke out of his trance and took off running as fast as his legs could carry him.

It was too late, though. The first guy out of the truck was bearing down on him at a full sprint, and undernourished Max was no match for the young, athletic construction worker. Before Max could get to the end of the alley and break away around the corner, he was tackled to the ground. Max thought he felt his collarbone snap.

One of the other crew members ran inside the printing business on the corner and called the police. Only a few blocks away, they arrived almost immediately. The police found Max being held face down in the alley by two of the construction workers. His face was bruised and his upper lip bleeding. The police never asked how Max had become injured. They cuffed him quickly. Max thought he felt his shoulder pull from its socket when one of the cops yanked him to his feet by the cuffs. They stuffed him unceremoniously into the backseat of the police car. The owner of the pawnshop watched from the back door of his store without saying a word. Within minutes, Max was being hauled away for murder.

Looking out the rear window as the police car turned from the alley onto the side street, Max had a feeling of déjà vu. Max thought about how quickly life could change. He thought about how much worse life had become for him since he was sent to juvenile hall.

6

17 JUNE 1977

Sometime before midnight . . . The music was loud, the throbbing beat was sexy, the crowd was sweaty, and Bill O'Reilly was hitting his groove on the dance floor to the Trammps' "Disco Inferno."

Disco fever was running wild across the country, and young O'Reilly was running as wild as anyone.

Dallas wasn't exactly the disco mecca that New York City had quickly become, but it did have the Beat Club. All of the cool young people in Dallas entranced by the disco craze made their way to the Beat Club to feel the music and hook up with other likeminded singles. Located in the loft of a renovated garment factory in a mostly abandoned industrial park, the Beat Club offered the extra thrill of slumming for the up-and-coming professionals of the area.

The Beat Club wasn't as sexually overt as Studio 54, but that didn't stop the kids inside from hooking up after hours or experimenting with copious amounts of the latest drugs. But young Bill wasn't drawn to the Beat Club for the drugs or the industrial setting; he went for the music, and if he happened to meet a willing girl, he was open to the opportunity.

Never wanting to look the fool, Bill had practiced several simple dance moves he had picked up from watching the Soul Train dancers on television. If he failed as a broadcast journalist, he thought, he might just try out for the show. After a few drinks he thought he might try out anyway. Not exactly a shy guy, Bill knew how to make the most of his limited dance moves under the disco ball and attracted a fair number of the fairer sex.

It had only been a few years before that that Bill could be found listening to The Doors, The Who, and Led Zeppelin. Like much of the country, though, when disco came to town, Bill could not refuse the sexy beats of Donna Summer, K.C. and the Sunshine Band, and Rose Royce.

On the floor that hot June night, Bill was at his best as the lights flashed under the glass floor to the beat of "I Feel Love" by Donna Summer. The super sexy song sung by the super sexy icon had Bill feeling the love with the rest of the dance floor.

Wearing a powder-blue sports jacket over a wide-collared pink button-down shirt with white jeans and white patent-leather shoes, Bill attracted a lot of attention from women seeking a strong male partner for the night. So long as they could hold a conversation, they had a chance with him. Being attractive was only the first barrier to overcome, as Bill was particular about the women he became intimate with. If all they had were a few dance moves to back up their good looks, they usually didn't get a second drink. After all, even in the swinging seventies, part of the attraction for any potential partner was an ability to hold an intelligent conversation.

At the time Bill was an up-and-coming television reporter for WFAA-TV in Dallas, and his on-air time had garnered him many female fans in the discothèques, such as the one who was currently dancing across the packed floor mouthing "I feel love" to him.

A woman in a purple jumpsuit had moved across the dance floor to make her move on Bill. She came in close and took his hands; he twirled her twice before pulling her back in close. Bill was intoxicated by her radiant sexual appeal. Everything about her screamed exotic. She had a wild afro sprinkled with glitter, wide almond-shaped eyes, long gazelle-like legs that in heels made her as tall as Bill, and high firm breasts nearly jutting out of her unzipped jumpsuit.

Bill and the woman danced to a couple more songs, spinning, grinding, and bumping. Their energy was electric. They drifted into their own world as the music pumped and the lights flashed and sex filled the air.

The couple finally made their way off the dance floor. Bill led her by the hand to his table. He motioned for a waitress. The woman ordered a drink; Bill ordered a Coke with ice in a short glass. When the waitress left with their order, Bill smiled at his new friend. She smiled back and leaned over the small table to say something in his ear. "I'm Ida Mae. What's your name, you tall, sexy devil, you?"

"Bill." Bill was smiling and staring straight into Ida Mae's eyes. He was glad the music was so loud; he didn't want to say too much.

Ida Mae said, "Bill, what do you say we blow this joint for someplace a little quieter?"

Bill was dizzy with excitement. He had never been with a woman like Ida Mae, so confident, so energetic, so straight to the point. The idea of leaving for somewhere a little quieter was a good one. Bill just kept smiling as he answered, "Sure thing, Ida Mae; that would be great."

Bill called his waitress over, paid the tab, including a generous tip. Arm in arm, with the music still pumping, the fevered couple left the Beat Club.

Ida Mae Johnson lived a few miles away in an upscale singles-only apartment complex. Bill followed her up the stairs to her third-story unit, unable to take his eyes off of her as she climbed the stairs.

At her door Ida Mae stopped, reached into her purse for her door key, and hesitated for a moment as she looked at Bill.

Bill could wait no longer. He slipped his hand around her slim waist and pulled her in close.

Ida Mae kissed him deep and slow on the mouth as she ran her fingers through his long brown hair. Still kissing, Ida Mae slipped the key in the lock and turned the knob. Going with his instincts, Bill kicked the door open and, still engaged with Ida Mae, walked her into the dark room and kicked the door shut.

=

Max Barnes was lying awake in the infirmary listening to the moans and groans of the other injured convicts surrounding him. He was silent even though he had been severely wounded on the yard earlier that day. It was one more time Max thought he would surely die. He took the injury and its pain in silence. Max had never been one to cry.

Max had been playing cards on the yard and had been doing something unusual: he had been winning. Max tended not to play cards because it was too easy to become indebted to another convict, and once one became indebted it was near impossible to pay the debt in full.

Often a simple cash debt that went unpaid meant having to submit to sexual favors at the debtee's request, and more often than not it wasn't even a request. Once the debt had been called and the debtor was unable to pay, the interest on the debt became the real issue. An unpaid debt with interest meant the debtor was essentially owned by the debtee.

When Max threw caution to the wind and decided to play cards and started winning, eyebrows were raised and suspicion took hold. Playing cards in prison was a true doubled-edged sword. Losing inevitably led to debt that led to unimaginable pain and suffering. But winning could sometimes be worse. Winners made easy targets for robbery. One had to develop a sixth sense in order to see trouble coming from behind. Losers sometimes suspected winners of cheating, and that tended to lead to unimaginable pain and suffering, and sometimes death. Convicts hate to be cheated.

Winning at cards might create suspicion, but quitting before giving the house ample opportunity to win its money back led to swift and vicious payback. There really were no winners in gambling in prison.

Max had been up fifty dollars when he decided to quit before his luck ran out. The house was silent; the signal had been given. Sign language was a silent and efficient mode of communication among convicts that only the most experienced guards could decipher. Max had become well versed in the secret language but had not mastered the art of seeing through the back of his head.

As Max walked across the yard, he carefully glanced in all directions, searching for the attack he was sure was coming. Looking left at two convicts playing checkers, ahead at a guard posted at the fence, and right at four members of a Latino gang, he suddenly felt the shank sink deep into his left side. The blows came fast and furious, six in all. The attack was over as quickly as it had begun. Max dropped to the ground, clutching his side and gasping for air.

His attacker continued walking toward the guard posted at the fence ahead without drawing any attention his way. Max never saw his face or his weapon.

Max was losing massive amounts of blood as he lay silently on the ground, dying. Nobody paid any attention. Max couldn't even call for help. As he lay on the ground, blood pooling beneath him, he wondered if karma was real, if reincarnation was real. Was he suffering the consequences of a previous life, one so evil he would know no peace in this one? Or would he return in a future life wealthy beyond his imagination for the injustices he endured in this life?

The guard finally saw Max on the ground, realized he was injured, and sounded the alarm. Even though Max was bleeding out, rapidly closing in on death, the guard would not approach Max before backup arrived. Guards were not supposed to break up fights or enter any unusual situation alone. Protecting the guards was the prison's first objective after containing the convicts; saving a dying convict was much further down the list.

By the time the area had been secured—only three minutes after the stabbing but what felt like hours to Max—he was unconscious. Max was taken to the infirmary. Although the medical staff was made up of certified professionals, their equipment was anti-quated, their working conditions not much better than a M.A.S.H unit's. Max was lucky; his internal injuries were not too severe. The penetrating blade had missed his vital organs. If his injuries had been much worse, he would have been transported to the local civilian hos-pital. He was lucky that that was not the case, because even though the civilian hospital was only a few miles from the prison, security protocol demanded a lengthy search process for all exiting transport vehicles, includ-ing medical, which could have delayed his treatment so much that he died in transport.

He didn't know his attacker, but that didn't really matter. A snitch he was not. He simply refused to answer any questions and would give no clues. Lying on the bunk in the infirmary, he knew that once he was cleared by the doctor he would be sent to the hole for not complying with the investigation. He would also receive a written violation that the parole board would use to keep him in prison longer. He knew the investigation was pointless. Prison officials would do nothing to the attacker anyway, and he would just be signing a death warrant that would be carried out in the most brutal fashion possible once he returned to general population.

For the time being, though, Max would enjoy the relative safety of the infirmary while his wounds healed.

7

15 JULY 1987

Bill O'Reilly hailed a cab outside ABC Studios in New York. He was heading to Mario's for a lunch of rare steak, roasted red potatoes, and red wine. He had just finished taping promotions for his segment on *ABC Business News Brief.*

Bill sat relaxed in the backseat of the cab as it inched along in the heavy traffic. The cab was on Park Avenue at East 106th Street, heading toward East Harlem and Mario's. As it crossed 106th, several shots rang out, the sound ricocheting between the crowded buildings.

The driver of the cab slammed on the brakes, causing Bill to throw his arms out in front of him to keep from ramming his head into the plexiglass partition. Bill shouted at the driver to stay calm as he whipped his head left to right, trying to see the shooter. Two more rounds were fired. The loud cracking of the gun left Bill's ears ringing.

Bill took a deep breath and remained calm. To his right he saw a group of people scattering like droplets of water on oil. A man burst out of the crowd waving a semiautomatic rifle, pointing it randomly at people running away from him. The crazed man drew a bead on a woman running toward Bill's cab. Her face was contorted in mid-scream when another shot cracked the panicked air. Her arms flew out to her sides as she tried to maintain her balance as the bullet ripped through her side, knocking her off her feet.

The injured woman cried out in pain and fear as Bill sat helpless in the back of the cab. People all around him were running for their lives, screaming and crying out for help. The crazed gunman fired several more rounds at random into the crowded street. Several people fell to the ground. Bill was unsure whether they had been struck by bullets or were ducking to avoid the gunfire.

From the relative safety of the cab, Bill got a good look at the gunman's face and made mental note of his hair color and length, his height and weight, and his skin color. If the gunman somehow managed to get out of the area alive, Bill would give the cops a good description for their sketch artist.

A few seconds later, more shots rang out. Now they were coming from several directions. The popping of rapid gunfire from different directions was disorienting. To Bill it sounded like a small army had descended on the crazed gunman and unleashed hellfire on him.

The New York City Police closed the perimeter around the attacker, who was prone in the street, riddled with bullet holes, blood soaking his dirty clothes and pooling around his body.

The police cordoned off the crime scene while they concluded their search of the area for other weapons and scoured it for shell casings. In less than a minute, four innocent victims had been killed in cold blood and the perpetrator shot dead by seven boys in blue. The man, a white male, possibly in his late forties, was not carrying identification. Police would never discover his motive for the bloody rampage.

Bill exited the cab and began walking back toward the studio, shaken but not injured by the tragic events. This scourge of society is what continued to motivate Bill to seek the truth, the facts, and to continue to press politicians to do their jobs.

Gun violence was out of control in his country, and he aimed to do something about it. Even after the attempted assassination of Ronald Reagan, the federal government was unable to enact meaningful legislation to control gun violence. Bill wanted these violent criminals removed from society. He wanted them to understand they could not continue to walk free.

==

Max sat on his bunk in the third gallery of 7-block in the Jackson State Prison and examined the scars he had accumulated over the years behind bars, behind the barbed-wire fence, behind the walls of the largest walled prison in the world.

He traced the arc of six puncture wounds along the left side of his ribcage where he had been shanked on the yard over a card game in 1977. The blows had come quickly and silently. He had almost bled to death that day lying on the ground in shock. Had the shank been a half inch longer, it would have punctured his lung. His assailant was never identified. Max had learned early on that to snitch on another convict was to issue a death wish.

He fingered the deep scar along his chin where he had survived being struck with a steel pipe in the machine shop where he had worked in 1979 stamping license plates. The attack had been in retaliation. The day before, Max had been attacked in the shower and defended himself with a shiv. The attacker lived, and the guards were not involved. The man he'd stabbed put a paid hit out on Max. Convicts preferred to handle matters themselves.

Max had received twenty-two crude stitches for the pipe injury, lost his job in the machine shop, and spent three months in the hole for his part in the fight. The scar didn't bother him so much. Visible scars were just survival badges for him.

Losing his job detail was what hurt him the most. The job had provided stimuli for his brain and action for his muscles, and even paid a small sum each month.

He eyed a thin red scar along his right palm. He had blocked an attack from a convict wielding a shiv made from a disposable razor blade in 1981. The attacker had accused Max of failing to pay a debt that had been transferred to him. Max had never borrowed from a convict. He'd learned early that once a convict owed another convict, he became his property—and that was a very bad thing to be. He had taken the blade from his attacker and sliced him along the back of his neck. Max was able to get away that time without being sent to the hole. His attacker held up his end by not ratting him out.

Over the years Max had been attacked for all kinds of reasons by convicts wielding all types of weapons. Even though he had not learned to walk with eyes in the back of his head, he did not walk in fear.

Examining the scars he had earned defending himself against some of the most crazed and dangerous convicts in the prison system, he was growing weary and tired of humanity. He wondered what he would do with himself if he were awarded parole this time.

In less than twenty-four hours, Max would be going in front of the Michigan Parole Board to explain why he had murdered a man fifteen years earlier, and to try to convince them he was a changed man, accepted full responsibility for his actions, and would not be a danger to society if he were released.

The first time he'd seen the board, they'd given him a twenty-four-month flop, stating they did not believe he had demonstrated a reasonable amount of remorse for his crimes. That day, when he returned to general population, he'd gotten into a fight that earned him a month in administrative segregation, the hole. That major ticket earned him a second twenty-four-month flop on his next trip to the parole board. He had learned his lesson then and had remained misconduct-free for two years.

Max had had high hopes of getting a parole on his third visit, but the parole board still gave him a twelve-month flop. In their denial statement, the board had claimed that he must have manipulated the system because he hadn't had any infractions in three years. They wanted to make sure he understood completely who was in charge. The unchecked power of the parole board to extend a convict's sentence was a force Max had become all too familiar with.

In his effort to prove he was worthy of his freedom, he had obtained his general education diploma, completed anger management therapy, and remained free of any major misconduct infractions since his last parole board hearing. Even so, he knew the odds of being paroled on his fourth visit were against him.

He hoped it would be his last time in front of the board. He didn't believe in God, so there was no point in praying for a parole. It didn't mean he couldn't hope, though. The lights on the rock went out. The maddening screams of the insane, the cackling of the crazy, and the singing of the saved began to ring out. Max folded his hands behind his head, crossed his feet, and closed his eyes and waited for sleep to take him away.

8

13 AUGUST 1997

Bill O'Reilly stepped through the brass and glass door of Nate's in downtown New York City. He stood for a moment, his eyes adjusting to the low lighting. He smiled and waved at the maître d', Maurice. Bill was a regular at Nate's, and Maurice revered Bill for his professionalism and charisma. Bill had a way of making everyone he came in contact with feel like they were the most important person in the room.

Maurice was expecting Bill; his dinner guest had already arrived. Maurice greeted Bill and escorted him to his table. Joe Laughlin, Bill's friend from childhood, stood to greet his old pal.

"Joe! How are ya, buddy? Glad ya could make it."

"You old son of a gun! You haven't aged a bit. What's your secret?" Joe had been using that rib for years and laughed every time as if it were the first.

"Come on, Joe, you know I can't reveal my secrets!" Bill appreciated the routine. It was their thing.

Joe and Bill had been meeting at Nate's every week since Bill had moved to New York. Maurice seated them at Bill's special table every time. They always ordered rare T-bone steaks, baked potatoes with brown gravy, and grilled peeled asparagus.

They talked for hours, laughing and getting along like guys half their age. It always looked as if the two had not seen each other in years. The conversation flowed freely, without interruption. Maurice always made sure the food was prepared exceptionally and brought out promptly and discreetly so as not to inter-rupt the momentum of the conversation.

Most of Maurice's celebrity patrons either didn't tip at all—some expected not to have to even pay for their meals—or they over-tipped to compensate for their rude, crass behavior. Bill was different; he tipped 20 percent, no more, no less. But it wasn't the amount of the tip that made Maurice look forward to serving him. It was the way Bill could lift a guy's spirits just by treating him with respect, like a man.

When Joe and Bill had finished their meal and dessert and had called it a night, Maurice hailed each a cab (as they always left in opposite directions). Joe hopped in his taxi and was quickly consumed by the dense traffic.

Bill turned to Maurice, shook his hand, and said, "Be well, my friend, till next time."

Maurice nodded and smiled and said, "Thank you, sir, I look forward to it."

=

Max Barnes sat on the loading dock of the warehouse where he had been working for the past year, eating a warm bologna sandwich from his brown bag lunch. It was the fourteenth low-wage job he'd had since being paroled nearly ten years earlier.

As he sat on the dock, chewing, Max thought about his station in life and wondered if that was as good as it was going to get for him. He knew no way to get above his circumstances. He kept to himself, taking every job offered, and worked as hard as he could.

Even though Max wasn't happy or optimistic and he wasn't sure things would ever get much better for him, he knew things could get much worse. Performing a physically demanding job, walking to work, and eating bologna sandwiches were far better than being in prison. They were also far better than being homeless and eating from dumpsters.

He wondered what it was that separated men. Why was one man born in luxury while another was born in poverty? Who decided which were blessed with riches, high-paying jobs, or amazing luck? Why were some beautiful people pure evil, and some undesirables pure saints on Earth? He also wondered how much a man could take before he snapped and just started killing people.

He'd had that last feeling a few times in life. He never knew what it meant or how he felt about it. Sometimes he just thought maybe some murderers were not really murderers but people who were unable to vent their anger or understand why they were angry in the first place.

Max swallowed the last bite of the dry sandwich, neatly folded the tinfoil it had been wrapped in, and placed it in the brown paper bag. Over the years Max had heard stories of Depression-era people who saved every scrap of paper, never threw away a single bite of food, and forever changed the definition of frivolous; as he folded the brown paper bag and slipped into his back pocket for the next day, he thought he understood where they were coming from.

He finished his bologna sandwich and went back to work.

9

9 AUGUST 2014

At 9:19 p.m. the man with less than four days to live was slumped on the stage of the Michigan Theatre, his face shattered, blood pooling.

One shot had cracked the dialogue, and for an instant the stunned audience fell silent. But as Bill O'Reilly was rocked to the floor, the entire place erupted in screams of panic and fear. Dennis, who just a moment before had been laughing at his friend's comments, succumbed to shock. He had been paralyzed with fear. His eyes darted left and right as the theater's full lighting snapped on. He was blinded by the sudden brightness, which only amplified his fear. He waited to feel the impact of a second shot and the searing pain that would follow. The second shot never came, though. After what felt like hours but was in fact only moments, Dennis dropped to the floor to tend to his friend. People were running in every direction trying to escape the unknown enemy.

Dennis knelt over his friend, afraid to check for a pulse and not find one. His doctor always pressed two fingers to his neck, on his carotid artery, but he couldn't bear to look at the hole in Bill's face. He closed his eyes and pressed his finger to his friend's neck, feeling for a sign of life. It was there, barely. Bill was alive. Dennis began yelling for someone to call 911 and shouted to the panicked audience, asking if there was a doctor in the house.

The 911 dashboard was already being swamped with frantic calls for help from frightened show-goers as they ran from the theater.

In seconds a man had rushed up to Dennis and pushed him aside, saying he was a registered nurse and that he could help. Behind him, several more people rushed in to help. Another male nurse pulled Dennis aside to check him for injuries.

The sounds of emergency sirens could be heard over the panicked din inside the theater. The historic building did not have the well-lit emergency exits of modern theaters, so the panicked audience funneled out the main entrance, pushing and shoving each other and causing a further bottleneck in the main lobby. People were jammed up from the threshold between the main lobby and the main seating area all the way to the front doors.

Paramedics had been idling in a nearby parking lot on call and were first to arrive to see hundreds of people scattering in the streets, running toward their cars or just running as fast as they could away from the theater.

Jackson City police officers were on the scene before the paramedics had made it out of their ambulance; they stopped the paramedics from rushing in blind before they had found out whether the shooter was still in the theater.

Time is always of the essence in a shooting. Trauma, blood loss, and damage to vital organs all mean emergency crews must act quickly at the scene, but the first responders knew if they came under gunfire they would be no help to whatever victims lay inside.

A minute later Jackson County Sheriff's deputies were on the scene. Michigan State Troopers were immediately behind them. The scene outside the theater was total pandemonium as sirens wailed and flashing lights glared.

Officers from all three agencies were on high alert as the terrified patrons ran from the theater, afraid for their lives. Many of them began shouting for help to the officers and pointing behind them at the theater doors.

The cops quickly went into action to secure the area. Following the police officers, paramedics wasted no time entering the theater to find the victims. They made their way through the last of the people trying to escape with their lives. The theater was awash in light as the gruesome scene played out on stage. Police officers surrounded the first responders as they approached the victim, clearing the off-duty nurses who had come to Bill's aid. All exits were covered, and additional officers fanned out through the theater to search for the shooter.

The paramedics acted quickly to assess Bill on the scene. He was barely breathing. He had lost a lot of blood, and his vitals were weakening. Contact was made with Allegiance Hospital officials, and the decision was made to transport O'Reilly by ambulance to the Allegiance helipad to rendezvous with the University of Michigan's Survival Flight American Eurocopter 155 B1 air ambulance.

=

Max Barnes jumped to his feet with the rest of the crowd as the theater erupted in chaos. Men and women looked around, wildly searching for the shooter. He could feel their eyes burning through him. He was sure they could now see the Ruger SR22 Rimfire pistol tucked neatly in the waistband of his jeans, the handle covered by his sweatshirt.

He too started frantically looking left and right and up to the balcony, where more screams could be heard. Max wanted to blend in with the panicking crowd and get out of theater as quickly as possible. Everywhere around him, people were screaming and pushing each other, trying to make their way up the aisle and to the lobby.

Max was shoved hard from behind by a large man in denim overalls and a black T-shirt. The man had been separated from his wife. He was calling a woman's name as he shoved Max from behind while reaching his massive arms across a row of seats to get his wife's attention.

In the chaos several people were trying to bypass the clogged aisles by climbing over the rows of seats. Another man had been dragging his wife by her arm over the rows when her foot slipped off the armrest, catching her ankle as she fell into the next row of seats. The woman cried out in agony. Max thought he could hear the tiny bones in her ankle breaking over the screams of the crowd as she writhed in pain.

The aisle was completely jammed, with everyone pushing as hard as they could to get the crowd through the narrow exit and into the lobby. Max felt the handle of his pistol jam into the back of a man in front of him. The man was too intent on getting to the exit to realize he had a gun poking him in his back.

Max lost his footing as he pushed through the crowd; he tripped on someone's feet and went down hard in the middle of the aisle. The push from behind him continued. Someone stepped on his hand. Others stomped across his legs. Max groped for the nearest seat to pull himself up. As he struggled to make his way to his feet, the Ruger SR22 fell to the floor. It was immediately kicked under a seat. Max tried to reach down for it before someone spotted it. It was too late. A woman making her way to the aisle between two rows of seats saw the gun and let out a scream of screams.

Max looked up and found himself looking straight in to the eyes of the screaming woman. He retrieved the gun and stuffed it back into his waistband. The wall of bodies was impenetrable. The woman continued screaming, but the audience had already turned into a frightened crowd fighting to escape eminent danger. Her screams were caught up in the chaos, and nobody else had noticed the gun or Max.

He couldn't believe he had dropped his gun and let someone see it. He knew the woman would be able to identify him. She had been so close, he could have reached out and struck her.

Max pushed his way up the main aisle of the theater with the rest of the crowd as emergency responders rushed down the service aisle on the south side of the theater. The woman who had spotted him and his gun was still stuck between rows of seats, unable to penetrate the clogged aisle. He fought to blend in rather than pushing past the rest of the anxious people. The congestion was worse in the main lobby because the audience members who had been watching the Boldest and Freshest show from the balcony were fighting to merge with the audience members from the main floor, and a massive bottleneck at the front doors had everybody jammed up.

People were pushing so hard to get through the main doors that some were pinned against the doorjambs under the crushing weight of the panicked crowd.

Still, Max continued struggling forward through the screaming crowd as bodies collided into each other. Just as he reached the main doors at the front of the theater, he could see the flashing lights of emergency vehicles. He could see an ambulance stopped under the marquee and several police cars surrounding it.

His heart was racing as he thought he would be stopped and frisked as soon as he passed through the door. But he pushed on.

For the first time in Max's life, he was thankful for his smaller physical stature as he crossed the threshold from the lobby of the theater onto the sidewalk and was able to blend in with the group of screaming escapees. He ducked slightly and ran along the sidewalk, passing close by a cop car and additional officers as they made their way to the front door.

Sirens wailed in the warm night air and lights flashed in an epileptic fit across the darkened sky.

Max turned the corner from North Mechanic Street onto West Pearl Street and headed west. He kept his head down and avoided looking at the police and emergency vehicles as they raced by en route to the theater. The streets were crowded with frightened people from the theater as onlookers joined in the fracas.

10

9 AUGUST 2014

The American Eurocopter 155 B1 air ambulance flew at an average speed of 175 miles per hour, covering the distance from Allegiance Hospital in Jackson to the University of Michigan's University Hospital in Ann Arbor in just twelve minutes.

The air ambulance landed in Ann Arbor and doctors rushed Bill to the emergency room. The highly skilled flight nurses had worked to stabilize Bill's vitals and began cleaning his facial wounds. Once on the ground at the hospital, they were able to give an initial report to waiting doctors about the nature of the wound, allowing the doctors to move quickly.

Doctors wasted no time prepping Bill for a computed tomography scan of his head to locate the bullet and assess the damage before surgery. Bill's vitals were weak, and he was losing strength with every passing minute.

The CT scan of Bill's brain showed a small-caliber bullet surrounded by bone fragments lodged in the temporal lobe of his brain. Immediately, surgeons moved Bill to an operating room to prep him for surgery to remove the bullet and as many of the fragments as possible.

While Bill was being treated for a life-threatening head wound, his friend and partner Dennis Miller had been taken to Allegiance Hospital. He was in a terrible state of shock, repeatedly mumbling the shooter might come for him next. He was sedated and admitted for overnight observation.

The Jackson City Police, Jackson County Sheriff's Department, and Michigan State Police had secured the theater and the surrounding area and begun the arduous task of interviewing as many people on the scene as possible, searching the area for discarded weapons, shell casings, and articles of clothing and tracking down a list of confirmed ticketholders. They also began compiling a list of area business owners who might have captured any of the action on their surveillance cameras.

The normally quiet city of Jackson had been turned on its collective ear as news of the attempted assassination spread quickly through each neighborhood. The streets were flooded with gawkers making their way as close to the theater as possible.

=

Max rounded the corner to his apartment. He had jogged and walked the just over three miles from the theater. Along the way, he wondered whether he should toss the gun in a trashcan, or maybe down a sewer drain. He knew he didn't want to get caught with it, but he decided to keep it anyway.

Back at his apartment, Max switched on his small television and immediately tuned in to the local news. News helicopters from the big three news networks were flying over the Michigan Theatre, zooming in on the police as they searched the area for the shooter.

Area residents had descended on the theater, trying to get a glimpse of the action. Police were working as hard at keeping the gawkers back as they were at keeping the witnesses at the scene in order to get their statements.

The helicopters provided a terrifying vantage point on the chaos with their shaky cameras, the sounds of their massive engines roaring and the propellers beating the night air. The scene at the theater was surreal for Max to watch on television after having been there only an hour ago.

In all of his planning, he hadn't accounted for what had happened. He was worried that the lady who'd seen him retrieve his gun would be able to identify him to police. He couldn't believe his bad luck at having dropped his gun and having had someone actually see it in the middle of all that confusion. Max just couldn't catch a break.

From the relative comfort of his tiny studio apartment, Max sat on his small lounge chair, his hand resting on the butt of the pistol still concealed in his waistband under his sweatshirt, and watched the scene unfold on the television.

Local news crews were interviewing members of the audience on the street. Each of them eagerly offered conjectures about who the shooter was and why he'd done it. They seemed to be inspired by the night's tragic events as they gave vivid descriptions of people they'd claimed to have seen carrying guns into the theater and of those they suspected were up to no good. They told the camera how they were praying for Bill to make a full recovery and hoped the shooting wouldn't stop him from continuing his television show or his live performances.

Max wasn't really surprised by everything these people were saying to the camera. He had noticed how people changed when the camera was on them. It was as if they were all suddenly thrown into the latest television drama and needed to deliver their lines. They wanted to sound informed and in the know. But most of all, they wanted to sound like good people, decent people who cared about the well-being of others.

11

10 AUGUST 2014

At 7:02 a.m. the man with less than three days to live was in the critical care unit of University Hospital in Ann Arbor, Michigan. He had undergone hours of intensive surgery to have the bullet and bone fragments removed from his brain.

The surgery had been successful, but Bill had slipped into a coma.

News crews had set up camp at the top-rated hospital with their satellite vans and power generators and their cords and lights and makeshift sets popping up like M.A.S.H. units. Reporters from the big three networks, along with reporters from cable news, Internet news sites, and even some print news organizations, were on hand to get the latest updates from doctors and interview supporters who arrived throughout the night and into the early morning hours.

The shooting of Bill O'Reilly had become an overnight news sensation. The city of Jackson practically doubled in population overnight as more news crews set up camp to get firsthand accounts and eyewitness testimony on the shooting.

Suddenly the sleepy little city in south-central Michigan was on the map. Everyone wanted to know what had prompted Bill to take his hugely successful stage show to a city no one had ever heard of before the shooting.

Images of the historic Michigan Theatre had been shown across the networks and appeared on the front page of the *New York Times*. Page 2 stories of the theater were in all the major newspapers.

The mayor of Jackson held a press conference to assure its citizens that they were safe from future shootings. The governor of Michigan held a similar press conference. It seemed like every public official connected to the city of Jackson and the state of Michigan wanted to reassure people everywhere that even though a high-profile celebrity had been gunned down in a crowded theater and no suspects had yet been named, people were safe to go ahead with their vacation plans of visiting the area.

The press met Dennis Miller at Allegiance as he was checking out; he refused to answer any questions. He was escorted to Jackson Airport and boarded a private jet home.

Meanwhile, Bill O'Reilly had become an overnight martyr. There was even a rumor that the Pope had sent a personal message to Bill and was planning a personal visit.

===

It had been less than ten hours since Bill O'Reilly had been shot in the face. Max was still in shock over the whole ordeal. All of the planning, the careful attention to details, and then barely escaping the theater after all hell broke loose. He wished he had never gone to the theater; he wished he had never heard of Bill O'Reilly.

He barely slept that first night; he kept hearing the sirens of the police cars and seeing their flashing lights. He had dreamed that he woke in Jackson Prison, convicted of murdering Bill O'Reilly. Several times he crept in the dark to his bedroom window and slowly pulled the curtain back, expecting to see police cars surrounding his apartment. Each time he was relieved that the night was still.

He sat engrossed in the Sunday morning news with the rest of the nation. Seeing the report that O'Reilly was in a coma was an interesting turn of events. Max wasn't an attorney, but he'd picked up a few things from the "jailhouse" lawyers he had met in prison. He knew there was a significant difference between attempted murder and murder one. He knew that difference hinged on whether Bill came out of the coma or died in it.

There was no sign of the witness on the morning news report. Max tried to distract himself by flipping through the other channels. He wondered if he was just being paranoid.

He wasn't surprised O'Reilly had survived being shot in the face at close range, though. Max had always thought Bill looked as tough as he talked. He thought Bill looked like he could have been one those mafia goons who was sent to break bones when people didn't pay their debts.

12

11 AUGUST 2014

A t 4:50 p.m. the man with less than two days to live was showing no signs of improvement. In fact, his condition had worsened and doctors did not know whether he would live through the day. He was surrounded by family and close friends. Fox News Channel had hired a private security firm to stand guard over him continuously.

Well-wishers and fans from all over the country had overrun University Hospital. Hospital staff had set up a separate room to hold the massive amounts of flowers being sent to Papa Bear Bill O'Reilly.

The Internet was abuzz with bloggers blogging about the shooting and calling for a nationwide grassroots manhunt. Obscure YouTube videos of the master debater had gone viral overnight. Fans from around the globe had posted their own tribute videos to Papa Bear. BillOReilly.com crashed when it was overwhelmed by demand for Bill O'Reilly swag. Thousands of Bill O'Reilly T-shirts were sold overnight.

JANE WHITE

Fans had flocked to the Fox News Studios in New York and California. Police and private security teams could barely contain the massive crowds.

The big three of the elite media group were running a smorgasbord of greatest-moments specials from O'Reilly's career as if he were already dead. Keith Olbermann wrote a heartfelt opinion piece for the *New York Times*. Fox News had been running nonstop clips from *The O'Reilly Factor* while promoting an in-depth three-part miniseries on Bill's turbulent career and his inevitable rise to the pinnacle of investigative broadcast journalism.

=

Max had gone to work that morning just like on any other. But it wasn't like any other day. One of the most popular men in the United States of America was in the hospital, in a coma. The air on his walk to work smelled different. With every car that passed him, Max felt another set of eyes staring at him.

When he punched his timecard, Max felt his coworkers watching his every move. All of the water-cooler journalists were talking about Saturday night's shooting at the Michigan Theatre. Everyone seemed to have an opinion, too.

Some people said Bill O'Reilly was a total prick, an arrogant S.O.B., and that he probably deserved whatever happened to him. Others openly condemned the shooter as a coward trying to bring down the only honest guy left in broadcast journalism. Nobody was in the

86

middle or without an opinion; people either loved Bill or hated him.

Max did what he did on any other day and kept to himself. He ate his bologna sandwich out on the steps and folded his tinfoil and bag and slipped them into his back pocket for next time. At the end of his shift, he punched out just as he did every day and walked home.

At home he sat on the worn-out lounge chair he'd purchased for five dollars at the nearby Salvation Army thrift store and switched on the television. He tuned in to the local news broadcast and stared at the screen. He thought the moment would come sooner or later. On his screen was a forensic artist's rendering of him, quite a reasonable resemblance. He knew his time was up.

A local reporter was interviewing a witness from the theater shooting. He watched with fascination as the woman who had screamed out in horror at the sight of his gun recounted her version of events into the camera. All through the interview, the sketch of his face remained frozen in the upper left-hand corner of his screen.

Watching the news broadcast, Max wondered whether anyone in his small building had ever paid enough attention to recognize him, and whether even if they did they would care enough to call the hotline and turn him in. In all the years Max had lived in the small studio apartment, he had never befriended any of his neighbors. He'd never initiated a conversation or waved or said hello. Whenever possible he even avoided eye contact.

For his entire life, Max couldn't remember ever having a single real friend. Real friends asked questions and always wanted to know more about a guy. Real friends wanted to share secrets and confess their thoughts and feelings. Max didn't want or need any of that.

He never sought female companionship, either. Max had gone his entire life without ever having a girlfriend. Having survived his abusive parents, multiple rapes during a year in the juvenile detention center, and then fifteen years in prison, Max had lost any desire he might have had to be with a woman. Max couldn't even remember the last time he'd felt any sexual desire, let alone had an erection.

For Max, life meant going to work and coming home to be alone in his apartment to watch television. After everything that Max had been through in his tragic life, that was just fine with him.

Ever since Max had run away from his mother at fourteen back in 1967, he had just wanted to be left alone. And now it seemed he was again in more trouble than he could manage.

There was no point in Max's trying to run or flee town. He didn't own a car and didn't have much money, and even if he had had a car and tons of money, he had nowhere to run and nobody to run to.

Max decided to do the only thing he could—wait for the cops to kick down his door and see where the bullets fell.

13

12 AUGUST 2014

At 8:00 a.m. the man with less than one day to live remained in a coma. Doctors were not optimistic that he would come out of it. They said there was simply no way to know whether he would recover from such a traumatic brain injury. Doctors told the media that the longer Bill was in the coma, the less likely it was that he would survive it.

The hospital had been overwhelmed by O'Reilly supporters and well-wishers and had to increase security threefold. It had set up a separate hotline to handle the massive volume of inquires that flooded the hospital phone lines. Thousands of e-mails poured in from people around the world seeking information about Bill's condition and offering to help in any way they could.

Back in Jackson, police had also been overwhelmed with calls to their hotline because of the sketch they'd released to the local news. Hundreds of people claimed to have personal information on the suspect, forcing police to sift through thousands of dead-end leads.

Community organizers had put together their own search teams. Bounty hunters, private investigators, and off-duty patrolmen were flooding Jackson to track down the shooter.

Gawkers and celebrity hounds had camped out around the theater along with the media. There seemed to be no shortage of candidates willing to tell their story of how the shooting of Bill O'Reilly had affected them.

The Jackson economy had seen a massive spike in revenue as motels and hotels were booked solid, restaurants were running out of food unable to replenish supplies quickly enough, and the local Oriental Health Massage Parlor was hiring to keep up with demand.

=

Max Barnes stepped out of his small apartment on Blackstone Street, fully expecting to see cop cars racing down the street, coming for him. He stopped at the sidewalk and looked to the corner to his left, then looked to the corner to his right. There were no cop cars coming for him.

He started the quarter mile from his home to his job at 211 West Monroe Street. As he crossed the street and turned onto Monroe, he heard a siren in the distance and his heart stopped beating. The siren was quickly getting closer. Max stood still, unable to lift his foot to take a step forward. He looked left, then right. Then the siren began fading again. Suddenly his heart was pounding in his chest. He lifted his foot and kicked it forward.

When he arrived he found his boss waiting for him at the door. He was standing with his arms crossed, cigarette clenched between his teeth. Max wasn't sure whether he should proceed. He figured he didn't have anything to lose, so he climbed the concrete steps.

His boss didn't say much; he didn't have to. He told Max to go ahead on and get things taken care of, and if by some miracle he didn't end up in prison for life, to come on back to work.

Max told his boss thanks and with a simple nod turned and walked back toward his apartment. He took his time walking the quarter mile. He thought about all the years he had spent in prison, the year he had spent in juvenile detention so long ago, and his parents who he hoped had both died slow painful deaths.

There was nothing left for Max to do but wait.

14

12 AUGUST 2014

A t 9:17 a.m. Papa Bear Bill O'Reilly, esteemed journalist, culture warrior, and American icon, was pronounced dead at University Hospital in Ann Arbor, Michigan.

The hospital's chief of public relations held a brief news conference on the main lawn to break the news to the public. More than a hundred reporters and journalists from across the country were in attendance. The mood was somber; only the clicking of cameras, the steady low-frequency hum of power generators, and the steady ringing of mobile phones could be heard.

For three days the number of supporters had steadily grown. Local hotels and motels were booked solid. Several RVs and buses were parked at the hospital. Camps had been erected on the hospital grounds. Fans had come from all over the country to show their support for their beloved television icon.

Despite the number of loyal fans who had shown up in support of their fallen hero, their culture warrior, Papa Bear had died from a single gunshot wound to the face and consequent brain damage.

After the initial shock of the tragedy sank in, the masses slowly began dispersing, loading their lawn chairs, cameras, and well-wishing signs into their cars, RVs, and buses and making their way home.

By noon the fickleness of humanity was evident, as the hospital was nearly back to normal. The news crews had cleared out, the fans had gone home, and security teams were relieved of their duty.

===

Max half expected the police to be waiting for him at the door to his apartment when he rounded the final corner. It was calm on his block. No police could be seen anywhere. He almost wished they were there. He knew they were coming.

At the door he paused, his hand on the doorknob. He listened for a moment. He heard a television in the distance, a dog barking even farther away, and the "beep" of a delivery truck in reverse close by. Max took a deep breath and opened the door.

He turned to close the door and stopped with just a slit of sunlight showing and looked down the street for any police cars. Again there was nothing. The street was quiet. He gently closed the door and locked it. He switched on the television and sat in his lounge chair to watch the news.

He watched with rapt attention as each channel replayed highlights from O'Reilly's career and showed taped interviews with several former colleagues and friends and neighbors. Max had watched as reporters interviewed some of O'Reilly's fans and supporters out-side University Hospital. He knew Bill O'Reilly had a loyal fan club and devout following of supporters, but he'd had no idea the numbers were so high.

One channel after the other had live reports from Fox News Studios, Marist College, Monsignor Pace High School, and Bill's childhood neighborhood in Levittown.

Tires screeched, doors slammed, combat boots tromped on the concrete. Max put a hand on the Ruger SR22 and stood, waiting to do battle.

PART TWO

1

Jackson, Michigan, was named after President-Elect Andrew Jackson—founder of the Democratic Party—and ironically is claimed to be "the birthplace of the Republican Party." The small rural town was founded by a frontiersman named Horace Blackman (also the namesake of nearby Blackman Township) in 1829. In honor of the newly elected "People's President," Horace called his new claim Jacksonopolis. "Jacksonopolis" turned out not to roll off the tongue so easily, and the name was changed to Jacksonburgh. By 1838 the name was simplified to Jackson, and it took.

The birth of the Republican Party took place when in 1854 a group of citizens assembled under an oak grove in Jackson and formally discussed politics as the Republican Party. It was that *formal* discussion that justified the title. One can easily imagine *informal* conversations of that nature taking place in several territories simultaneously as the country established its political footing. And, in fact, *formal* meetings just like that one were happening across the country, giving at least three other cities claim to the same title.

There hasn't been much public debate about which city is the actual "birthplace" of the Republican Party. The title is mostly used by Jackson's tourist board for marketing. It is also trotted out by local Republican candidates during campaign season when they're looking for some intangible connection to the people, something that can't be judged against them, a non-issue to inspire their base.

Locals give little thought, if any, to the green road signs touting the city's heritage that they pass as they drive along I-94 and US 127. The historical significance is mostly used in elementary schools and local libraries in an effort to boost the city's image with the next generation. Unfortunately, each generation cares a little less.

When Bill had read about the four cities all claiming to be the birthplace of the Republican Party, he'd booked dates for his Boldest and Freshest show in all of them. The stop in Jackson was the last of those four cities, and Bill was excited to finally get there.

Bill thought it was a great venue. He liked the historical significance of the city and the theater and was very much looking forward to doing his show there.

The Michigan Theatre was situated on Mechanic Street in the heart of downtown Jackson. It had first opened its doors in 1930 and had hosted some of the most popular vaudeville acts of the era in its heyday. Locals had often dressed in their Sunday best for big Hollywood movie premiers. As it was the first building in downtown Jackson to boast air conditioning and offered the attraction of spending an afternoon with people's favorite Hollywood stars, the theater had been a major draw for area residents.

By the 1970s the famed theater had fallen into a state of disrepair and closed its doors in 1978. Fortunately, the theater had escaped trendy renovations over the decades, and much of its original glory was intact when it was purchased in 1993.

Since then, the theater had undergone renovations and restoration projects and reopened its doors to a new generation. In its reincarnation, the theater hosted classic films celebrating the history of Hollywood, popular animated films for children, and cult classics such as *The Rocky Horror Picture Show.* In order to continue raising funds, it began hosting theater performances as well as concerts and stand-up comedians. The Boldest and Freshest Tour was the biggest act to come to the theater in a decade and had promised to be the most popular.

2

Marian Hurley had first met Maxwell Brown during the summer of 1965. He had just returned home from the Michigan State Police Recruit School. He was excited to start his new job as a Michigan state trooper. When he stepped off the Greyhound bus on Main Street, he saw a beautiful young woman walking out of the drugstore a few doors down the block.

The proud new graduate pulled his shoulders back, raised his chin, and walked straight up to her and introduced himself. Marian shook his hand as she gazed into his eyes. He offered to buy her a soda. Maxwell and Marian had spent the rest of that first day together talking about all of their hopes and dreams. Maxwell courted Marian through the winter, and they married in May 1966. Marian wanted nothing more than to be a wife and mother.

Jill Maxine Brown was born in the small rural town of Hillsdale at the Hillsdale Community Health Center on 17 November 1966. She would be an only child.

Her parents doted on her, especially her father. Maxwell cherished his daughter. He often read to her in the evenings and made up heroic stories of state troopers saving the day. He didn't want his daughter to know the real pain and suffering of the job he did every day.

From the time Maxie (her father had always called her Maxie) could walk, he took her fishing at his favorite fishing hole. Not long after, he taught her to ride a bicycle. When she was ten he taught her to hunt. At twelve she joined the junior rodeo and the 4-H Club. At fourteen he taught her to drive the old Ford truck around the property. Her father was there for her through each milestone. Jill not only loved her father, she admired him.

Jill had been fifteen when her father was killed in the line of duty. He was shot in the back while attempting to execute an arrest warrant on a suspected bank robber. Jill was devastated. When she turned sixteen, she decided she too wanted to be a Michigan state trooper. She knew no better way to honor her father.

Jill Brown graduated from the 101st Michigan State Police Recruit School in 1987. Immediately after graduation she began her career as a trooper at the Jonesville post in Hillsdale County.

Jill was a no-nonsense trooper. She was sympathetic to victims and merciless to perpetrators. As a rookie, she had earned the nickname Lightfoot.

She earned the nickname after one particularly memorable incident early in her career. While on patrol one night she had pulled over a pickup truck for speeding. There were two passengers in the truck. She radioed in the stop and had just opened her door to exit her patrol car when both suspects fled on foot. Using her lapel mic, she radioed in that she was in foot pursuit of both suspects. They had fled in the same general direction and had a few-second lead. Jill gave chase to suspect 1 first. He was in his early twenties and athletic, but Jill was prepared. She had been training for this moment her whole life. Within seconds she had closed the gap to about twenty yards and was gaining quickly. Suspect 2 had broken off and jumped a fence and was heading down an alley. Closing the gap to a few feet, Jill had repeatedly ordered the man to stop. Within one stride she dove and made a bone-crushing tackle. She attached one cuff to the suspect's wrist and dragged him about ten feet on his back to a telephone pole, cuffing him to it in a bear hug position.

With one suspect down, she radioed in that she was now in foot pursuit of suspect 2. She vaulted a fence and sprinted down the alley. She had lost only a few seconds immobilizing suspect 1 and was homing in on suspect 2. Following the sound of barking dogs and the sight of motion-activated lights, Jill closed in on her man in just a couple of blocks. She caught a visual when he ran out of the shadows to cross the street. She could hear his ragged breathing as she closed the gap. Coming at a full sprint from his blind side, she lowered her shoulder and drove the man hard to the ground. But suspect 2 was not going to surrender as easily as his partner. The man struggled to get to his feet. He didn't want to fight; he wanted to run. Jill had her backup cuffs ready, though. With one quick motion, she slapped one cuff on his right wrist and the other on his left, and then drove him face first back to the ground.

When her backup arrived a few moments later, she was already walking suspect 2 back to suspect 1, who was cursing himself for not being able to outrun a girl.

Jill was able to outgrow her nickname as she continued to excel at her job. Over the years she worked hundreds of dangerous cases. She caught drug dealers, pimps, rapists, and murders. She counseled battered women, helped teen runaways rebuild family ties, and made extra stops at homes of seniors she knew lived alone to make sure they were OK.

Over the years she had gained the respect and trust of her colleagues and climbed steadily through the ranks. In 2011, when budget restraints had forced a reorganization of the entire Michigan State Police, including shutting down many of the posts and restructuring the rest, Jill was promoted to inspector. Accepting the promotion, though, meant relocating to the Jackson post.

Jill had decided to move to the city of Jackson to get to know her community better. She and her life partner had bought a beautiful home on ten acres only two miles from the post. The couple was happy in their new home, and Jill was thriving in her new position.

3

Jeannie Redmont had been born to Eunice and Roy Redmont on 26 October 1947. Eunice gave birth at W. A. Foote Memorial Hospital in Jackson, Michigan.

Roy was a toolmaker who ran his own small but successful tool-making company in town. Roy was a proud man, a loyal friend, and a patriotic citizen.

Eunice taught Sunday school and was a dedicated wife and mother known for her cooking skills.

Together, Roy and Eunice wanted to raise their daughter with integrity and discipline. They read to her, talked openly with her about politics and religion, and kept a strict watch over her social life.

Jeannie was an active Young Republican at the age of twelve. While her peers were fascinated with television and the Beatles, she was fascinated with Richard Nixon and the Grand Ole Party.

Her father, a staunch Republican and anti-Democrat, gave her a copy of Barry Goldwater's book *The Conscience of a Conservative* for her thirteenth birthday. Jeannie devoured the book the way other girls devoured Nancy Drew novels. She kept it on her nightstand for years, often referring to it when she felt confused or out of touch with her peers.

Jeannie was a proud Goldwater Girl. With money she earned walking dogs and babysitting, she purchased her Goldwater Girl/Cowgirl outfit, complete with the AUH$_2$O sash and straw hat.

As a freshman in high school, she had run for student council and lost. It was a tough defeat for her to accept. She knew her opponent was only in the race because she was popular with the boys. Not willing to give in to defeat, Jeannie regrouped as a sophomore, putting together a solid campaign and winning the election. Once on the council, she upheld her campaign promises. Her peers respected her integrity. She was elected class president as a senior. Jeannie took her role as president very seriously. She knew her peers counted on her to represent their needs. Jeannie wanted to be the voice of the voiceless.

As class president Jeannie had dreamed about going to college and maybe running for public office afterward. She thought of how much good she could do for her community if she were elected to the city council, or as mayor.

But Jeannie's dreams were dashed before she could even apply for college. As class president she had attracted the attention of several boys. She had become smitten with the handsomest of them all, Richard. He had asked her to senior prom, and she wondered if life could get any better than that moment.

Prom night, in the heat of the moment, Richard had convinced Jeannie she had nothing to worry about.

Jeannie, wanting nothing more at that moment than to make him happy, had acquiesced. Richard had not believed a girl could get pregnant her first time having intercourse. Shortly after senior prom, it became clear to him she could.

Jeannie considered abortion despite her religious beliefs. She knew she was too young to have a child. She wanted to go to college and have a career. She kept the pregnancy secret from Richard, wanting to solve her problem on her own. She believed it was mostly her fault for getting pregnant in the first place.

Jeannie's mother was the first to discover her secret. Mothers always know. Jeannie hadn't thought about her lack of use of tampons. It was simple math. Her mother had cried and screamed and cried some more before telling her husband that their baby girl was going to have a baby.

Jeannie's father took the news a little better. At least he didn't cry and yell. Her father went to Richard's house and talked to his father. Jeannie and Richard were married the following Sunday at the local Baptist church. It was a nice ceremony, mostly family. A small reception was held in the church basement.

There was no official honeymoon for the newly-weds. Jeannie and Richard moved into the basement of her parents' house while they saved for their first apartment. They moved out of the basement two weeks before their first child was born.

Jeannie's dream of running for public office was never realized. She accepted her role as housewife and mother with regret. She raised four well-mannered girls and kept a spotless house. Jeannie never burdened her family with her woes.

Richard had learned to weld in high school and was accepted as an apprentice after graduation. He went on to become a journeyman welder. With the assistance of his father and Jeannie's father, he opened his own welding and fabrication company. Richard ran a successful business and provided a comfortable living for his family.

4

Billy Barnes had a reputation as a troublemaker all through school. He fought with his peers, sneered at the girls, and disrupted class when he was bored. Billy made it through high school because he could play baseball. He was an all-star pitcher. His coaches didn't care what he did outside of baseball as long as he showed up on game day.

As a freshman he learned his coaches would make sure he passed all of his classes so he could keep playing ball. Each year he put less effort into studying and more into playing. When he graduated he had no discernible skills and no offers to play college ball. For his eighteenth birthday, his old man told him he was a bum and threw him out on the street.

Billy crashed on a friend's couch while he looked for work. Within a few days he found a job at the Coney Island Café in downtown Jackson, Michigan. He started as a dishwasher. When an opening for a short-order cook came up, he asked for the job and got it.

Ruth Blakely dropped out of high school at fourteen. Insecure and lonely, she had fallen for an older man, a gym teacher willing to exploit his authority, and her naiveté for his benefit. She had been having sex with her teacher because she thought he loved her and wanted to marry her. When he told her he thought she understood he was married, and that nobody could ever find out about their relationship, she was heartbroken and embarrassed. The day he broke her heart was her last day of school; she put all of her books in her locker and walked home.

When she got home that day, it was obvious to her mother that something traumatic had happened; Ruth's eyes were puffy and red from crying. Her mother questioned her briefly and gently. When Ruth refused to talk about it, her mother stopped pushing. The following morning Ruth woke as if she were going to school but got ready to look for a job instead. At the breakfast table she told her parents that she had quit school and had decided to get a job. Ruth's parents didn't much believe in education. Having grown up in the Great Depression, they valued employment over schooling. Ruth began waitressing at the Coney Island Café in downtown Jackson a week later.

Billy had worked at the Café for two years when Ruth started. Ruth Blakely made an immediate impression on Billy Barnes. From the minute he first set eyes on her, his goal was to charm her out her pants. Despite his reputation for being a hoodlum, she agreed to go out with him. Before Ruth's affair with her gym teacher, she'd believed a person shouldn't have sex with another unless they were both in love. Her heart now broken, she decided love and sex were not compatible.

On their first date, Billy took Ruth to the drive-in theater. He wasted no time getting her in the backseat of his car. Billy was rough with her, groping and squeezing. He was nothing like her first lover, who had been kind and gentle. Billy knew what he wanted and wasted no time in going for it. Ruth was frightened and begged him to stop. Billy thought it was all part of the game.

For the next week at work, Ruth avoided Billy as best she could. By the next weekend, though, he had convinced her that he'd really thought she liked it and that if he'd known she really wanted him to stop, he would have.

Ruth and Billy went out every weekend that first summer. They drank and fought and had sex. By August Ruth had her first black eye from Billy. He apologized and told her he only hit her because he was so crazy in love with her that he couldn't help himself.

By October 1953 Ruth had moved into Billy's room at the boarding house. In March 1954 Ruth discovered she was pregnant. She went to her parents and persuaded them to let her marry Billy. Ruth's parents didn't want to get stuck with a pregnant mouth to feed, so they agreed to the marriage.

Ruth and Billy continued working at the café and rented a small mobile home before the baby was born. Being pregnant didn't stop, or even slow down, their drinking, smoking, and fighting. The more visible her pregnancy, the more violent Billy became.

Billy didn't want any children. He wanted to party. And he didn't need any extra mouths to feed. Life was hard enough just taking care of him and Ruth.

One night Billy came home drunk on whiskey and looking for a fight. He had been brooding over how having a baby was going to ruin his already pathetic life. He stormed into the mobile home and yelled for his wife. He found her in bed crying; she knew she was going to get a beating.

He dragged her off the bed by her foot. With Ruth screaming on the floor, he kicked her in the stomach. As she lay on the floor, curled up in pain, he went to the closet and got a wire clothes hanger. He waved it around as he yelled at her and told her that if she wasn't going to have an abortion, he would do it for her.

Before he could act out his threat, someone pounded on the trailer door. One of Billy's drinking buddies—misery loves company.

On 28 September 1954, Max Barnes was born. Billy was at a bar getting drunk. But Billy wasn't getting drunk to celebrate the birth of his child; he was getting drunk to forget the birth of his child. While his young bride was in the hospital pushing out his baby all alone, Billy was hooking up with a two-bit bar whore.

Ruth left the hospital with her baby the following day, and Billy nowhere around. Billy didn't come home for three days. When Billy finally came home, he was still drunk—and mad. That night he wanted to have sex with Ruth, and she refused. He'd always known that child was going to ruin his life. He raped her.

5

William James O'Reilly Jr. was born 10 September 1949 to Winifred Angela Drake O'Reilly and William James O'Reilly, Sr. He was born in New York City, the greatest of great cities. In 1951 the family moved to Levittown, New York. There they grew into the quintessential working-class Irish American family.

William Sr. was a working-class guy who understood the value of a dollar. He wasn't exactly niggardly, but he was certainly frugal. He never purchased a new car; secondhand cars served his purposes just as well. When it came time for the family's annual sojourn to Florida, they left the driving to Greyhound.

Winifred did her part, too. She clipped coupons, saved her Green Stamps, and pinched pennies wherever possible. She made sure the lights were off when nobody was in the room and had a deft touch metering the thermostat through the harsh New York winters. Luncheon meats were commonly the special of the day. She also packed brown sack luncheons for those treacherous bus trips to Florida.

Bill O'Reilly and his younger sister, Janet, grew up swimming in the local municipal pool with all the other hoodlums of the neighborhood during the dog days of summer. They spent their share of days running the streets and causing just enough trouble to be noticed without getting themselves arrested. In the winter Bill got his exercise throwing snowballs at passing cars and running to avoid the wrath of angry drivers.

Just like the aboriginal people of Australia, who never missed having indoor plumbing because they never knew it existed, Bill and Janet never missed flying in jets or swimming in private pools. Despite their humble childhood, they were healthy and happy.

William and Winifred provided the foundation on which their family could build healthy, meaningful lives. Young O'Reilly was raised to know the harmful effects of drinking and smoking and knew that abstinence was the only way to stay pure. He learned to treat all with women with respect and dignity. And he learned the value of building lifelong friendships.

Bill's parents also thought that playing it safe in life was the best route. Get a good education. Get a decent job, one you can retire from with a nice pension. Marry a nice girl or boy. Don't drink too much. Don't gamble. Stick to the basics and you'll do just fine, because just fine was really pretty good.

Bill's working-class lineage was well documented: His maternal grandmother had been a telephone operator, one grandfather a Brooklyn cop, the other a train conductor, and his uncle was a fireman. His father worked as an accountant. His sister became a nurse, and in the beginning Bill became a teacher, just as his parents expected him to.

Winifred and William Sr. both had college educations, but not for the same reasons Bill wanted one. Winifred and William Sr. thought college was where one went to get enough education to get a good middle-of-the-road job. It was a chance to play college sports, to be recognized for one's achievements. The O'Reillys and their peers went to college, went to work, raised families, and basically remained in their neighborhood with little interest in climbing the socioeconomic ladder. William Jr. had a different idea of what college was and what it meant to others.

William Jr. realized even before he went to college that the privileged few knew that college was about much more than textbooks and exams and weekends at home. They knew about experiencing life and its riches firsthand. They knew the benefit of college abroad. The Privileged knew that a person who wanted to see the landscape of the world needed to travel rather than looking at pictures. And they knew that a person who wanted to experience other cultures had to immerse himself in those cultures in person rather than reading about them.

When Bill Jr. told Bill Sr. he wanted to study abroad, his father nearly choked on his potato stew. Sr.'s biggest concern was that Jr. would miss out on making the baseball team. Jr. recognized at that moment how small his father's world had become. The impact of his father's words would stay with him for the rest of his life.

The paradigm shift Bill experienced that day would shape his views on family, tradition, standard of living, quality of life, and socioeconomic class relevance.

6

Jeannie had voted in every presidential election since she turned eighteen. She had tried to follow politics as closely as she could while raising her family. She had read the dailies in the early years of her marriage, and paid close attention to her local news.

When she and Richard upgraded to cable in the eighties and Jeannie saw CNN for the first time, she was fascinated by the available content. She became an avid watcher of cable news. But even with cable and CNN, Jeannie was still searching for something else, something more.

As cable news evolved, Jeannie was along for the ride. She was absolutely beside herself when she first saw the Fox News Channel. When *The O'Reilly Factor* debuted, she knew she had found that something else she'd been searching for.

As her children grew up and moved out, Jeannie spent more time following her favorite broadcast journalist, Bill O'Reilly. She never missed an episode of *The Factor*. On those occasions when Bill O'Reilly used a guest host for a day off or a vacation, Jeannie always compared the substitute's performance against her idol's. They never lived up to his standard.

Each time Bill released a new book, Jeannie bought it. When she finished reading each book, she went online and posted reviews on dozens of reader-generated blogs, chat rooms, and Amazon.com. Even though Jeannie always posted very favorable reviews of Bill's work, they were not puffery. She really could not find fault in his work and was genuinely happy to tell anyone who would listen how she felt about it.

If Bill asked his audience to donate to a particular charity, she did. If he asked his audience to boycott a certain store or product, she did. When Bill told his viewers, "Don't take my word for it, look it up and see it for yourself," she did.

Jeannie found Bill's "word of the day" enlightening and useful. She kept a handwritten log of each word. She would write the definition next to it and then write three sentences using the word. The next day she always tried to incorporate his word of the day into her conversations.

Jeannie was Bill O'Reilly's number one fan. She was a member of the Bill O'Reilly Fan Club and president of her local chapter. She logged onto BillOReilly.com every day for bonus footage from *The Factor* and behind-the-scenes stories about Bill's guests.

Jeannie Redmont and her husband had been watching *The Factor* for nearly twenty years when O'Reilly announced he was bringing his show to her hometown. She absolutely adored Bill O'Reilly. When she heard the Boldest and Freshest Tour was coming to Jackson, she went online and purchased her tickets. She desperately wanted to meet the man in person, so she ponied up the $1,400 for two VIP tickets that included a meet-and-greet after the show with Bill and Dennis. For weeks leading up to the show, she couldn't talk of anything else.

The night before the big show, Jeannie made a scrapbook to commemorate the event. The day of the big show, she woke early and made Richard breakfast in bed. In the hours before the big show, she still had not been able to decide which Bill O'Reilly book she would take to be autographed. In the final hour before the big show, Jeannie decided to wear a Bill O'Reilly "Culture Warrior" T-shirt to have it autographed. She planned on having it framed afterward to display in her living room. After she'd worn it to bed a few times, that is.

By the time Jeannie finally made it to the Michigan Theatre and took her seat, she was ecstatic. She had her smartphone so she could take plenty of pictures.

When Bill took the stage, she nearly piddled in her slacks. Few moments in her life had been that exciting.

Jeannie sat with her husband and watched her idol only a few feet away from her, up on the stage. She was in awe of him. She had always thought he was handsome on television, but in person he was so tall and even more handsome than she'd realized. His powerful voice resonated like music in her ears.

Using her smart phone, Jeannie snapped several pictures; careful not to be rude or intrusive, she kept the phone low and had the flash off. After taking the pictures, she remembered that her smart phone was also a video recorder and switched modes. The recording would of course be for her personal viewing. She did not want to violate any copyright laws.

Unfamiliar with the video-record mode on her phone, Jeannie fumbled with the touch-screen controls to focus the tiny lens. As she touched the screen to begin recording, a shot rang out.

When Jeannie heard the shot and saw Bill fall to the floor, she screamed in horror. She simply could not believe such a horrible thing could have happened. Jeannie didn't realize she had dropped her phone in the commotion. When she realized there was a killer in the theater and that she might be shot too, she jumped to her feet and tried to escape with everyone else.

The frightened crowd began rushing for the exit. Richard had been seated to Jeannie's left; when they jumped up to escape the theater, Richard was behind Jeannie, struggling to reach the main aisle on their right.

With Richard pushing her from behind, Jeannie worked her way between the rows of seats toward the aisle. At the main aisle, with Richard still pushing from behind, Jeannie was too frightened to force her way into the aisle. Bracing herself between Richard and the tidal wave of bodies crammed shoulder to shoulder, Jeannie saw a man drop to his knees in front of her and fumble on the floor for something.

To her amazement and horror, she saw what he was for reaching for: a gun. She recognized it as a pistol with a silencer. As the man retrieved the gun and began fighting to get to his feet, he looked up and straight into Jeannie's eyes. She screamed as loud as she could to alert everyone of the killer, but her screams were drowned out in the mayhem.

Richard continued pushing from behind. Jeannie made into the aisle some twenty bodies behind the man with the gun. As she pushed and fought her way up the aisle and into the lobby, Jeannie tried to keep her eye on the man. In the lobby the man pushed hard through the crowd and made it out into the night and disappeared before Jeannie could see which way he went.

7

For fifteen years Max had lived in relative peace and quiet in a cramped studio apartment. He had paid his rent on time every month and never asked the superintendent for a thing. Max went to work and returned to his apartment to watch television. That was his routine. Lay low. Don't draw attention.

The low-income building he lived in hadn't had cable access when he moved in, so Max had watched whatever was on the local channels. At first he passed the time watching the evening sitcoms that depicted beautiful young white people all seemingly having a great time in life no matter what happened to them. Those shows quickly wore on him; rather than helping him escape reality thirty minutes at a time, they just made him more aware of his own pathetic existence. When he discovered network game shows, he decided that although most of the contestants seemed happy enough, they must have been desperately unfulfilled to subject themselves to such humiliation for a chance at a few bucks. He wondered whether there was any limit to what people would do for money. Soon enough those shows wore him down too, with their perfectly coiffed hosts and runway-model assistants.

With nothing but time and a television for company, Max was left with the local news. He had avoided the news for so long because he knew the bad things people did to each other. But day after day he walked home, put a pot of water on to boil for his macaroni, and tuned in to the news. After a while he realized that watching the news was a passive way to see the action but be safe from its consequences. He became fascinated by the escalation of violence and the insanity of the world. He was constantly amazed at the levels of pain that people intentionally caused each other. Every day it was the same dirty news: house fires and burglaries, armed robbery, drugs, gangs, kidnapping, rape, shootings at school and at work. Max thought it was a wonder humanity had survived as long as it had.

One day while Max was tuned in to the six o'clock evening news, there was a knock at the door. It was the building superintendant. He told Max the property management company that owned the building was finally upgrading to include basic cable access.

Max had never seen cable television. At first he was upset about the rent increase that would come along with the cable installation. Then the day came when his television was connected to the service; Max was overwhelmed by the number of channels. That initial awe soon wore off when he realized most of the programming was low-budget mindless entertainment, half-hour long commercials, and reruns.

What Max did like about cable was the access to the news channels; he hadn't even known channels dedicated to airing only news existed. And there was more than one. Max hadn't thought there was enough news to fill one channel all day every day, let alone several.

It became an addiction of sorts for Max to watch news from the time he walked through his apartment door until he couldn't keep his eyes open. He often fell asleep in his lounge chair.

It didn't take long for Max to see that each news channel told the same story from a completely different perspective. Sometimes the news channels told such wildly different versions of a story that Max was sure they must be reporting on different stories altogether.

Everyone, Max decided, had an agenda. He wasn't sure what that agenda was, but that didn't stop him from feeling overwhelmed by the bias of it all.

One time, a power surge in his building caused the screen on his television to go black. He could see his reflection in it. The image was surreal; he was watching himself watching himself. He felt pathetic. Contempt for the image on the screen crept over him. He began to feel unsure of reality. When the power flickered on a few seconds later, he could still see the outline of his image superimposed on the screen. He threw the paper plate loaded with macaroni and cheese at it.

Even as his contempt grew for the people who delivered the news through his cable box, he continued to watch. He marveled at their arrogance and narcissism. He wondered what they were like when the cameras were turned off. What did they talk about at home, with their family and friends?

Then Max happened across *The O'Reilly Factor*. The format for the show was different from the others, just a guy and his guest. No special effects, six-person panels, or fluff pieces. Just hard news facilitated by a no-nonsense host.

Max had finally found a news guy who didn't mince words or follow popular opinion just for the sake of ratings. Max sensed a self-made man. Max felt like he could relate to the guy, like the guy understood Max's position. For Max, the guy represented what was right with the world. He felt the guy was fighting the good fight.

But then Max noticed something else about the guy. Because he watched the guy every day, he began to see a pattern. He saw the guy belittle women, condescend to certain activist groups, minimize civil rights violations of certain races. He saw the guy blatantly lie about the president and other politicians he didn't agree with. It was all very hard for Max to understand. He started to see a pattern of hypocrisy on a level he had never seen before. Max felt betrayed again.

Max felt more impotent than ever. Day in and day out as he watched the guy, Max grew darker on the inside. He started taking notes, making a journal of things the guy said about people, the offhand racist remarks, the lies. He didn't know what he would do with the journal, but he felt he couldn't just let the guy keep getting away with it.

He was getting old, and he knew his health wasn't good. He couldn't remember ever being seen by a real doctor. Max felt that if he was going to redeem his life, he had to do one great thing before it was too late.

He collected news articles and magazine clippings. He fantasized about killing Bill O'Reilly. He would have to go to New York City, but that would take a lot of money and he didn't even know how to find him once he got there. For months Max ruminated, angry and impotent. Then he heard the guy announce that he was coming to the Michigan Theatre, just a few miles away from Max's ghetto apartment, and he knew he had to take action.

8

Bill and Dennis landed at Jackson Airport an hour before the show was scheduled to begin. They had chartered a private jet because of their demanding schedules that required they waste no time slogging through a major airport. Jackson Airport was only five minutes from the Michigan Theatre. Bill and Dennis would have plenty of time to get to the venue and freshen up before show time.

Jackson Airport was tiny, no doubt, but the staff was used to high-profile celebrities flying in on their private jets. With the Michigan International Speedway only minutes from the airport, many top NASCAR drivers used it to avoid having to fly into Detroit Metro Airport and then make their way through seventy miles of perpetual construction and interstate congestion.

Bill walked quickly across the small tarmac and through the gate to his waiting car. There were no paparazzi or news media, no red carpet or velvet ropes. There were no fan lines or autographs to be signed. It was all very smooth and trouble-free for Bill and Dennis.

Rather than commissioning a limousine or one of those giant gas-guzzling SUVs for the three-mile drive, Bill and Dennis shared a hybrid taxi. Bill rightly thought SUVs were at the heart of many of our country's economic and environmental problems. Bill didn't understand flashy, luxurious cars when the goal was only to get from point A to point B.

A block away, they noticed the crowd gathering for the show. Bill was always humbled by the huge turnout at his shows across the country. He was just an average guy who worked hard like anybody else. He appreciated every one of his fans who spent hard-earned dollars to come to his show. Sure, the tickets were expensive, but they were worth every penny.

They pulled into the alley and stopped in front of the security team. The alley was quiet and dark. Bill and Dennis were escorted into the theater through the rear door. Bill was a master of his game and did not need to warm up or get jazzed or psyched or pumped. He met with a few of the theater workers and the security detail, and reviewed the post-show schedule of meeting VIP guests and signing autographs. The cue for the show to start was given, and Bill and Dennis shook hands and headed out on stage.

There was no warm up act for the Boldest and Freshest Show. Bill preferred to get straight to business.

9

nspector Jill Brown was in her pajamas, curled up on the couch with her life partner and a dime-store mystery novel, when she got the call. It was 9 August 2014, and her captain was telling her there had been a shooting at the Michigan Theatre during Bill O'Reilly's stage show.

The Michigan State Police were always on alert when a high-profile national celebrity was in town. When Jill heard that Bill O'Reilly was coming, she had imagined the crazies would come out in droves. She knew O'Reilly was a polarizing character and that there would be an equal number of fanatics at each pole.

Jill hung up the phone and told her partner she was sorry—again. Work was work, and Jill's partner knew and accepted the challenges that came with loving a cop. Jill quickly changed into her uniform, ran to her patrol car, and radioed dispatch that she was en route.

When she arrived at the scene, she felt like she'd arrived late to a party that had gone tragically wrong. Downtown Jackson was lit up with dozens of flashing lights from police cruisers and rescue vehicles.

Jill passed through the groups of people huddled in groups outside the theater. Officers from the Jackson City Police, the Jackson County Sheriff's Department, and the Michigan State Police were taking statements and searching the area.

Jill made her way into the theater, where dozens of officers were searching for anyone still in the building. Jill joined in the search. The theater had a seemingly endless supply of nooks and crannies large enough for a person to hide in. Even with the large team of officers searching, it took over an hour before the all clear was given.

The search for physical evidence came next. The theater was evacuated of all nonessential personnel; just the small team of investigators was left. The team systematically covered every square inch of the cavernous theater.

Early in Jill's career she had sometimes been surprised at the items she found at crime scenes, especially ones involving such a large crowd all fleeing simultaneously. After more than twenty-five years on the job, though, nothing surprised her. The team had found several mobile devices, purses, wallets, and articles of clothing. She supposed when one was running for one's life, those things just did not seem as important anymore.

It was early morning when one member of the team began a sweep of the projection room on the main floor. The projection room door didn't lock and hadn't been used for the stage show. The room was well organized, uncluttered. The investigator took his time, making sure he covered every square inch. On the floor, wedged under the baseboard, he found a .22 caliber shell casing. The only substantial clue the team had found.

With all of the evidence bagged and tagged and the action having died down, Jill drove around the city, thinking. The shell casing was on its way to the forensic lab to be analyzed. She made a mental note to call University Hospital in the morning. She needed to know whether they had been able to remove the bullet from the victim. She would also need to see x-rays of the entry wound to help determine trajectory. If she could determine exactly where O'Reilly was at the moment of impact, it would help narrow down where the shot had been fired from.

In her career Jill had found plenty of shell casings unrelated to her crime scenes. That was another thing that used to surprise her. She used to wonder how many gun crimes went unreported. Finding the shell casing in the projection room would only be a single piece of the puzzle.

She had a lot of questions about what had taken place at the theater. The initial information was too fragmentary to make sense. Some witnesses claimed they heard one shot, some two shots. Some witnesses claim the shot they heard sounded muffled, some claimed the shot was deafening. Some witnesses claimed to have seen a muzzle flash, others claim there was none.

Jill thought about returning to the scene of the crime to do her own evidence sweep. But that was not how she operated. She trusted her coworkers; they were all good cops and good at their jobs. She knew it was just her desire to catch the bad guy feeding her impulse. After all, they had found the shell casing.

What she needed to do was go home and get some sleep. What she did was go back to the station. She had a lot of work to do. There was the arduous task of sifting through the reports and statements from the scene. Also, she wanted to know if any serious threats had been made against O'Reilly.

Assassinations were not crimes of opportunity, she knew. They were crimes of intent. Someone had to have spent some time planning the shooting and the escape.

10

Jill returned to her desk the night of the shooting to review the statements collected from witnesses. She read through each statement carefully, parsing each sentence, trying to make sense of the senseless. There were always inconsistencies from witness to witness, she knew. People remembered details in their own way and expressed them in their own way, too.

Where one person had heard a "pop," another heard a "bang." Where one person had seen a "flash" of light, another saw a "shimmer." Where one person had heard everyone else screaming, others heard only themselves.

Early on Sunday, 10 August, Jill was handed a statement from a witness who claimed to have actually seen the shooter. The witness, Jeannie Redmont, had spent the night at the hospital with her husband. He had been injured trying escape the melee. Jill was tired, exhausted really, but she read the statement carefully and decided she needed to speak to the witness immediately.

Jill tucked Redmont's file under her arm and headed for her car. Redmont's house was less than ten minutes from the station. She considered calling ahead because of the early hour but decided against it; she wanted their initial meeting to be in person.

Jill stopped her car in front of Redmont's house; the sun was up, and she was beat. With the file in hand, Jill approached the house and knocked on the door.

Jeannie Redmont answered surprisingly quickly. Jill had half expected Redmont to be sleeping, as she'd had a long night at the hospital with her husband. She figured Redmont must still be amped up on adrenaline.

Jill introduced herself and asked if she might step in for some follow-up questions. Redmont was only too happy to oblige.

Inside, Jill asked Redmont to tell her what she'd seen and heard at the theater. Rather than get right to the point, Redmont began by telling Jill a little about herself. She talked about her interest in politics and how one thing had led to another and she'd happened upon *The O'Reilly Factor* and how that Bill O'Reilly had changed her life. Jill was patient; she had interviewed more witnesses than she could remember, and they all had their story to tell. It seemed to Jill that many of them had been talking without an audience for a long time.

Midway through her monologue, Redmont apologized for her poor manners and offered the inspector a cup of coffee. Jill politely declined. Redmont resumed her account.

When Jill sensed that Redmont was losing track of her story, she gently coaxed her to the night in question. Redmont apologized, telling Jill that so much had happened so fast with her getting tickets, and Bill being shot, and her husband getting injured, that she was just having trouble sorting it all out. Eventually she got around to how she'd come to see the suspect and his gun. Redmont's second version—much like that of nearly every other witness Jill had ever questioned— varied slightly from the first.

In her original statement, Redmont had claimed only to have seen the man retrieving a gun from under a seat and then disappearing into the crowd. In her retelling of the facts to Jill, Redmont claimed to remember more details after having had some time to consider everything that had happened.

The inspector knew that some witnesses did gain clarity after calming down and having a chance to reflect on a situation; she also knew that others began to embellish certain details in order to somehow seem more important to the case. And Jill felt the latter was going to be the case with Redmont.

Redmont now claimed to have seen the suspect drop his gun, too. And as a matter of fact, she said, she'd seen him carrying it in his right hand as he pushed his way through the crowd. When Jill asked Redmont whether she was positive she'd seen him carrying the gun, Redmont feigned indignation. She said not only had she seen him carrying the gun, but she'd also seen him hit at least one man over the back of the head with the butt of it to get through the crowd faster.

Jill knew that the more times Redmont told her story, the more embellished it would become. She wanted to know about the gun. She asked Redmont if she was familiar with guns and whether she had been able to determine what caliber it was.

Redmont told her all she knew about the gun. It was small, black, and had a silencer. Redmont said she knew it had a silencer because the gun barrel had flat sides except for the two inches or so at the end.

Jill was confident now that the shell casing hadn't been left behind from some other random, unreported gun crime or teenage mischief.

All she needed from Redmont now was for her to cooperate with the forensic artist to get a composite drawing of the suspect. She told Redmont she would have the forensic artist come over as soon as possible.

Having heard enough, Jill thanked Redmont for her time and excused herself. Without looking back, she got into her car and sped away.

From her mobile phone, she called in to have the forensic artist dispatched and was told there would not be one available until the following morning at the earliest. Jill knew the longer it took for him to get there, the more Redmont's imagination would take over. Jill would have to worry about that later. She ended the call to dispatch and remembered she'd wanted to call the hospital.

11

Jeannie watched Inspector Brown walk to her car and drive away. She didn't much like the tone the inspector had taken with her. She knew what she'd seen, and if the good inspector wouldn't listen to her, well then she knew who would.

She went to her purse to get her mobile phone to call her friend and neighbor. When she picked up her purse she immediately sensed it was too light. She quickly unzipped it and started rummaging for her phone. Before she got to the bottom of her purse, she remembered she had dropped the phone when she heard the shot in the theater. There was no time to worry about her mobile phone now. Jeannie needed to talk to her friend; she would figure out how to get her phone back later.

She picked up the phone in her kitchen and dialed her friend and neighbor. Jeannie repeated the entire story, going all the way back to when she first saw Bill O'Reilly on television and knew he was special. A pot of coffee and two hours later, Jeannie's confidant told her she should tell her story to the local news channel.

She told Jeannie the news loved to get involved when the police weren't doing their job.

This was Jeannie's chance to stand up for what was right, and to be on television. She went to her computer and found her local news channel's website. In three clicks of the mouse, she found the "contact us" button and typed out a quick e-mail describing the events of the night as she saw them.

Within minutes of clicking "send," Jeannie's phone was ringing in the kitchen. A producer from the local news channel said he would love to hear her side of the story, a real first-person account. He said the channel had interviewed several other witnesses from the scene but that none of them had actually seen the shooter.

The producer had a soft voice—relatable, Jeannie thought. She felt like he was on her side, that he believed her. He told her how lucky she'd been to get out of there alive. He told her how sorry he was that her husband had been injured in the chaos. He told her that if there was anything he could do for her personally, to please call him any time.

Jeannie told him she was more than happy to do a live, on-camera interview with his station. She told him to go ahead and send a reporter over, that they could do the interview right from her living room. The producer thanked her and confirmed it was OK to shoot the interview live from her living room, then told her he was dispatching a camera crew immediately.

Jeannie said, "No, no, give me an hour to get ready." She reminded him she'd had a long night at the hospital and needed to freshen up before going on camera and all. Before the producer disconnected the call, he told Jeannie just how brave she was for going on air and telling her story.

As she replaced the phone on its cradle, Jeannie Redmont was absolutely glowing. She needed to get ready for her big moment.

12

Jill decided that calling the hospital could wait. She knew she needed sleep to do her job. As she drove past the station en route to her house, she called in to let them know she would be back in a few hours. Jill knew she could have just stopped there in person, but she also knew it wouldn't be so easy to get away.

Jill brought her car to a stop at the end of her long driveway. Ann, her best friend and life partner, was sitting on the porch steps drinking pink lemonade. Her heart sank. She had left Ann last night and had not even called to say hi since she left. Jill loved her job, but it was moments like this that made her doubt how strong that love was.

Sleep came quickly as Jill met her mattress face down. Ann was generous in so many ways; giving space to Jill when she was overworked was just one of them.

It was late afternoon when Ann finally woke Jill; she hated to wake her after so little sleep, but Jill had told her it was important that she get back to work. After a quick shower, a tuna sandwich, and a glass of that pink lemonade, Jill was back in her car and on her way to the station.

At her desk she remembered she still hadn't called the hospital. She pulled the number up online and called. The surgery, she was told, had been a success. Doctors had removed several bone fragments and the bullet, but O'Reilly had slipped into a coma. She knew that if he died it would change the case. The bullet had been turned over to the Michigan State Police early that morning.

Another phone call revealed that the bullet had been sent to the forensic lab, along with the shell casing found at the scene. A call to the lab revealed the bullet was a .22 caliber long rifle. The bullet was too deformed to confirm a match to the .22 caliber casing.

In the movies the weapon of choice seemed to Jill to always be a 9 mm semiautomatic or a .45 caliber revolver. Bad guys in movies never tried to take someone out with a .22 caliber; it just wasn't macho enough. But Jill knew how lethal a .22 caliber weapon could be in the hands of the right person.

Jill removed Jeannie Redmont's file from the pile on her desk. She flipped to Redmont's statement and read the part where Redmont described the gun. A small black pistol, semiautomatic, silencer. It could have been the weapon. The .22 caliber long rifle bullet could be fired from hundreds of weapons—rifles and pistols alike.

One more call that Jill wanted to make was to Bill O'Reilly's manager. She knew outspoken celebrities like O'Reilly were the frequent recipients of threats of all kinds, including death threats. Most of these threats were basically harmless; sometimes people just wanted to vent their misguided anger at a celebrity. Jill had seen plenty of these types of threats from drunks and cowards. The problem was in determining which of the threats were legitimate before someone acted on one.

In the O'Reilly case, Jill already had a victim. Now she needed to find out whether a threat had been made.

Her team had done an excellent job of gathering information, and she quickly located O'Reilly's manager's mobile phone number in the file. She punched in the number and was surprised to hear a voice on the other end before the first ring had finished.

Jill was not surprised when the manager told her that Bill O'Reilly had received death threats on a near-daily basis. He said that they came in every conceivable fashion. Jill thought she heard him chuckle a little as he described them. Some came in Bill's private e-mail. Some were sent through Fox's website. Some crazies still neatly typed their threats and signed them at the bottom with "Sincerely yours," "Affectionately yours," or "With love." Others, the ones wanting to live out their favorite movies, cut letters and words from dozens of magazines, then glued their message to a single sheet of typing paper and dropped it in the mailbox.

In the end, after nearly an hour on the phone with the manager, Jill had decided that none of those threats would ever be carried out. These days, she knew, people had a tendency to voice their opinions in the form of thinly veiled threats. Before she ended the call, though, she asked if he would forward her copies of all the threats Mr. O'Reilly had received over the past month. She wanted to look them over just in case something specific to the scene of the crime popped up.

13

The Channel 6 news crew showed up at Jeannie's house late Sunday evening. She had waited all day. The nice producer on the phone had told her they would be over that morning. When they finally came to her door, she was mad, but not mad enough to blow her chance to be on television. The crew offered their apologies for their timing, claiming there had been some other important breaking news they'd had to cover first.

Jeannie welcomed the crew into her home. She'd thought the crew would be bigger. It really wasn't a crew at all, just a cameraman and a nice news lady. In her head *news crew* sounded more important. She decided that when she told the story to her friends, it would be *news crew*. No reason to explain, she thought.

As Jeannie and the nice news lady chitchatted, the cameraman set up the lighting and wired the two women with lapel microphones. The nice news lady would still hold a stick microphone in her hand. It was all about the look for her.

The nice news lady was pretty and spoke in a high-pitched, singsong voice. She smiled a lot at Jeannie and said,

"You have a beautiful home here, Mrs. Redmont."

"Do you think, really? Oh, thank you. It really is our dream house, you know." Jeannie was blushing.

"Those shoes are adorable! You must tell me where you got them," the nice news lady gushed as she touched Jeannie's arm.

The nice news lady told Jeannie she wanted her to just loosen up and relax a bit before they began recording. She talked to Jeannie for about ten more minutes before they began rolling camera. Jeannie was ready. She didn't need to relax, or want to. She wanted to get on television. She wanted to tell her story. She wanted Inspector Brown to see she wasn't making it up. The public would sympathize with her. They would call her and tell her how brave she was for telling her story with a killer on the loose.

For forty-five minutes, Jeannie talked while the camera rolled. The nice news lady had asked a couple of open-ended questions that allowed Jeannie to tell her story with little interruption. Jeannie told her the whole story, from the beginning. She relished the attention.

The nice news lady hoped she would have five minutes, six tops, of usable footage. Two minutes of that would be cut for promos and teasers. She told Jeannie her story would run the following evening. She asked Jeannie if she would be available for a follow-up story then and maybe a short on-air interview. Jeannie of course offered to help in any way she could.

She thanked the news crew for coming and showed them the door. She'd done it. She was going to be on television, and maybe even live!

14

Around noon on 11 August, Jeannie Redmont welcomed the forensic artist into her home. She was nervous. She had been telling the story to her friends and family since yesterday morning. She hoped she could accurately describe the man she'd seen with the gun after describing him so many times already.

Jeannie offered the man a cup of coffee or a glass of water as he set up his kit. He told her thank you, no. He was fine. The man was calm, professional. He told Jeannie to just relax and he would do the work.

Jeannie hadn't known what to expect, really. She thought she was going to describe the man she saw with the gun and the forensic artist would take her description and put it on paper. Easy. That wasn't so.

The forensic artist asked dozens of questions about each of the man's features. He asked her about the bridge of his nose, the shape of his nostrils, and did he have visible nostril hair. He asked about the man's eyelashes, the color of his eyes, the shape of his eyes, and the contour of his eyebrows. Was he wearing glasses? Was he thin? How long was his hair? Was it combed back? Did he use hair product? Were his teeth white? Were they straight or crooked? Were his lips thin or full? He asked about the shape of his ears, if his lobes were dangling, and if they were pierced. Did the man have any facial hair, or was he clean-shaven?

The questioning and the drawing went on for hours. Each time the artist drew a feature, he showed Jeannie and asked if that was it. He took his time, altering their shapes and repositioning them.

Jeannie was exhausted. She did the best she could to remember. She felt a weight of responsibility to get the details correct. When the artist stopped asking questions and stopped drawing, he showed the sketch to Jeannie and she was amazed at what she saw. It was the man with the gun. No doubt.

The artist thanked her for her time and cooperation and packed up his kit, and Jeannie showed him to the door. She watched him leave, drained but excited.

She went to the kitchen to make a sandwich and remembered she hadn't called about her phone. She decided that before she made her sandwich and forgot about her phone again, she would call Inspector Brown.

15

Jill had spent the day reading the hundreds of death threats that had been sent to Bill O'Reilly over the past month. His manager had forwarded them first thing that morning with a simple note attached that read, "Good luck." She'd thought she had seen it all. She was shocked at the vitriol and hatred one man inspired. In a macabre kind of way, she was even amused at the creative ways people threatened to take his life.

There were the hands-on guys, the real emotional ones who threatened to choke the life out him with their bare hands. There were the gore-seekers who threatened to hack him to pieces with an axe. There were the wannabe gangsters who wrote things like "swim with the fishes," "cement shoes," and "worm food." There were the ones who wanted to play the "expect the unexpected," "sleep with one eye open," "watch your back" game. There were the torture enthusiasts who threatened to shove all manner of implements of destruction in every orifice, pull his fingernails off, and poke and prod him to death. There were more than fifty of

155

them who just wanted to waterboard him for the fun of it. There were also the ones who wanted to tie him to a chair, cut his eyelids off, and force him to watch the Clintons' vacation reels on a loop and read Hillary Clinton's autobiography to him. In the end Jill decided none of the threats were from her man.

It was late in the day when Jill got the drawings from the forensic artist. She studied the face on the page, memorizing his features, looking into his eyes. It was a troubling face, no doubt. She saw pain, and anger, she thought. But she wasn't sure she saw a murderer. She had copies made to distribute throughout the department, to send to the other cooperating agencies, and to release to the press.

Jill was considering heading home for dinner with Ann before the sketch was aired on the evening news; maybe she could catch a short break before the phone lines were flooded with leads. She knew it would make Ann happy and help recharge her batteries.

Before she could commit, though, her mobile rang. It was Jeannie Redmont. Jill didn't waste time with pleasantries, and Redmont didn't seem to notice. Redmont told Jill about how her mobile phone had been left behind at the theater. She began telling Jill that her daughter had bought her the phone as a gift and went into a lengthy backstory about learning how to use it and all of the excellent features it had. Then Jeannie stopped abruptly. She remembered she had just started recording a video of Bill O'Reilly when he was shot. Redmont told Jill about how she took a few pictures even though she wasn't supposed to and how she even began recording a video just before the shot rang out.

Jill couldn't believe what she was hearing. This might be the lead that broke the case wide open. Jeannie Redmont might have filmed the shooting, or the shooter, or both. Jill told Redmont that if her phone had in fact been left at the theater and had in fact been recovered, that it would have had been tagged as evidence and would not be released until the case was closed.

Jill got a description of the phone, then ended her call with Redmont. She wanted to check the phone for pictures and video. The phone would be in the evidence locker.

She rushed to the evidence room—a thousand-square-foot room packed from wall to wall and floor to ceiling with boxes, bags, and envelopes full of personal effects, drugs, weapons, cash, etc.—and signed in. The officer on duty directed her to the evidence collected from the theater shooting. Everything was clearly labeled and organized. She had no trouble locating the phone among the thousands of items.

The phone was in sealed plastic bag. Jill removed the phone and pressed the power button. Nothing. Damn it. The battery was dead. Jill had an idea. She quickly snapped the back off the device and found what she was looking for: the memory card. She removed the memory card and asked to use the officer's computer.

Jill was surprised by how elevated her heart rate had become. She was anxious to view the pictures and watch the video. She inserted the card and clicked on the photo cache file. Jeannie Redmont was a prolific picture taker. She had hundreds of unnamed photos. Jill let out a long sigh; this was going to take some time.

16

The nice news lady from the day before showed up at Jeannie's house a few minutes before the evening news was set to air. Jeannie was expecting her. She was a little disappointed to see it was still only the nice news lady and her cameraman rather than an actual news crew. Oh well, she was going live on television in a few minutes, and that was all she really cared about.

The Michigan State Police had released the forensic artist's sketch of their main suspect, and the nice news lady wanted to interview Jeannie live when it debuted. She told Jeannie it would be great TV.

Inside Jeannie's house the cameraman set up his lighting and pinned lapel microphones to both of the women. The news lady would again hold a prop mic for effect.

The segment began with two minutes of the taped interview from the night before. Jeannie watched herself on the small television she kept in the living room; the sound was muted. The moment was surreal. Here she was about to go live on television as she sat watching herself on television.

When the cameraman gave the signal that they were live, Jeannie was suddenly overwhelmed with the realization of what she had survived and began crying. The nice news lady ignored the tears, looked into the camera, and said, "We're here live with Jeannie Redmont, survivor of last Saturday night's shooting at the historic Michigan Theatre in downtown Jackson. Friends and neighbors in this close-knit community have flooded Jeannie with love and support in her attempt to overcome her brush with a crazed gunman. You see, Jeannie Redmont came face to face with the man suspected of shooting Bill O'Reilly that fateful night. She has bravely come forward to the police with her statement and a description of the suspect. Showing now in the corner of your screen is the police sketch of the suspect. Police have issued a warning: the suspect is considered armed and very dangerous. Do not try to apprehend him or approach him. Police are urging anyone with information regarding the suspect to call the tip line at the number showing at the bottom of your screen."

Holding the prop mic up to Redmont's face, the nice news lady said, "Mrs. Redmont, you were at the Michigan Theatre Saturday night, correct?"

Jeannie was not expecting the softball question but answered anyway. "Yes, my husband and I had VIP tickets to see Bill O'Reilly."

The nice news lady was smiling widely, nearly giddy with anticipation over the sensational details Jeannie Redmont was about to describe to her live audience. She turned to Jeannie. "Mrs. Redmont, can you tell us exactly what happened that night, what you saw?"

Jeannie was staring into the camera lens. She drew a deep breath to stifle her tears. She said, "It was the scariest thing I've ever lived through. When I heard the gun go off, I nearly jumped out of my seat. Then I realized Mr. O'Reilly was shot. He sort of slumped out of his chair and landed on the floor. It was surreal. I had been watching Mr. O'Reilly on the TV for years and there I was finally seeing him in person, and *blam*! He gets shot smack in the face!"

"Mrs. Redmont, what happened after the shot was fired? I can only image the terror everyone inside the theater must have felt at that moment." The nice news lady was holding the prop mic up to Jeannie's face but looking at the camera, and smiling, just a little.

"Oh yes, dear Lord, it was total pandemonium. People started screaming and jumping over the seats, and everyone was pushing to get out before the gunman opened fire on'm. Me too. And my husband Richard. We were scared as anyone and just wanted out of the theater. You know, it was crazy, all of a sudden that big ole theater felt about as small as a walk-in closet. "

"It really sounds terrifying, Mrs. Redmont. How did you and your husband escape?"

"Well now, that's when I came face to face with the guy . . ."

"You mean the gunman?" The nice news lady's eyes were a little too wide with excitement.

Jeannie looked at the camera, then at the nice news lady, and then back at the camera and said, "Yes, the gunman. I came face to face with him when I was pushing my way to the main aisle. I was pushing, Richard was pushing from behind me, and we get just about to the main aisle and this guy in a gray hooded sweatshirt drops to the floor in front of me. Well, I look down at him and he's scrambling around, reaching under the seats. So I looked around the floor and there it was; the gun he used to shoot Mr. O'Reilly."

"So you saw the gun that was allegedly used to shoot Bill O'Reilly?"

"Yes, I did. I saw the gun. It was a pistol and it had one of them silencers on it, you know, like you see in the movies. And, well, I looked at the gun, then at the man, and right then he looked up at me, right into my eyes. He looked just like the devil, I say."

"Did he say anything? What happened next?"

"Well, I screamed as loud as I could. And long, too. I could have won a screaming contest right then, I screamed so loud. But it didn't matter because everyone was screaming. Nobody even looked my way to see why I was screaming."

"That sounds horrifying."

"It was. It was. After I screamed I got real mad and wanted to stop the maniac from escaping, so I pushed my way into the aisle and tried to follow him. I got real close, too. I nearly caught up to him. But he got through the main doors and disappeared before I could get outside."

"And where was Richard during all this action?"

"Oh my! I almost forgot! Richard had been knocked down and nobody even tried to help him up, and they all just tromped over him, the poor thing. He had to go to the hospital for his injuries."

The interview was over in two minutes. The entire segment was only five minutes. The nice news lady urged the audience to call the tip line at the bottom of their screen or visit the station's website and follow the special link that had been set up if they had any information at all regarding the identity of the suspect in the sketch.

Jeannie Redmont felt a rush of endorphins as the light on the camera went dark and the cameraman started packing his gear. She felt a pang of regret that the interview had passed so quickly.

The nice news lady thanked Jeannie for her cooperation and told her she admired her bravery. Jeannie was beside herself. She was actually blushing as she walked the cameraman and the nice news lady to the door. She was even disappointed when she opened the door for them that there weren't others on her lawn waiting to interview her, no neighbors waiting to catch a glimpse of her.

17

Jill had to click through hundreds of useless pictures before she got to the ones taken at the theater. There were only five pictures taken that night. The first one was of the marquee announcing that Bill O'Reilly was performing there. The second was of Jeannie and her husband, Richard, under said marquee. The third was of an unidentified man on the stage with a microphone; Jill guessed he was the show's emcee. The fourth was a nice shot of Bill O'Reilly as he crossed the stage. And the fifth was of Bill O'Reilly sitting in his stage chair, smiling. Jill thought there must have been plenty of women who thought he was ruggedly handsome; he reminded her of John Wayne in *McLintock!* Neither photo of O'Reilly showed any audience members. They were both zoomed in on Bill.

The last file on the memory card was the video. Jill wasn't a particularly superstitious person, but she crossed her fingers anyhow. She clicked to open the file. She could hear Bill O'Reilly talking, some light laughter from the audience, but the video only showed a pair of ladies' feet in sensible flats and the chipped-paint floor. The video was unstable, shaky. It whipped up to a blurred shot of the stage, then back to the floor. Jill could hear a rustling sound and what sounded like a person mumbling to herself. Again the video shot up to the stage and back to the feet and the floor. The third time the camera went up to the stage, it stayed there, out of focus. Bill came into focus for a moment, then went right back out. Again the focus was adjusted but missed its mark. Then, just as the focus was being adjusted for the third time, the shot came. Instantly the view from the camera went sporadic, up to the ceiling then clanging around on the floor.

It was as Redmont had told her: just as she began recording, the shot had been fired and she'd dropped her phone and fled.

The video would be of no help. Jill slammed her fists on the desk. She played the short segment several times, trying to get some useful audio from it. One more time through, and she realized she could hear the shot clearly. Redmont had described the gun the suspect picked up as having a silencer. Jill had believed that part of the description because Redmont had described the flat sides of the gun barrel versus the rounded shaft of the silencer. Redmont had clearly been mistaken, though.

Jill removed the memory card from the computer and replaced it in Redmont's mobile. She signed out of the evidence room and headed back to her desk.

Back in her office, she called the forensic lab to have the rest of the mobile phones analyzed for pictures and video. Maybe someone had had better luck capturing some useful footage.

After a few minutes at her desk, she got a call from her captain telling her the forensic artist's sketch of the suspect had just been shown on the evening news and the tip lines were already lighting up.

Jill leaned back in her chair, drew a deep breath, and exhaled slowly. She was in for another long night of following up on leads. She stayed in her office until well past midnight working on the case. She finally relented and went home when she realized she had again forgotten to call Ann.

18

On Tuesday, 12 August, Jill was back at her desk before sunrise. Calls to the tip line had been pouring in steadily through the night.

At her desk she took the tall stack of leads and began sorting them. There were the ones she referred to as "Elvis sightings," the ones that were too fantastic to be real; those went into the "useless" pile. There were the ones from "the regulars," the ones that came from shut-ins, paranoids, and conspiracy theorists who called in to the tip line every time something happened; those went into the "highly unlikely" pile. Then there were the few that seemed to have some validity, the ones from callers with coherent speech patterns, able to actually speak in complete sentences and provide specific details; those went into the "follow up" pile. It wasn't a perfect system by any means, but it seemed to work for Jill, and it was too late in the game for her to work on a new one.

Jill sat thumbing through the short stack of leads to follow up on when she heard a light knock on her door. She looked up to find Ann holding a cup of coffee and a plate covered in tinfoil. Jill smiled and stood to greet her. She had left early without waking Ann or eating breakfast. There was an ache in Jill's heart at the sight of her. Ann seemed to always be thinking of Jill's best interest. Jill loved Ann for that too; Ann knew Jill hadn't eaten and cooked her breakfast. Jill's stomach growled as the scent of butter-fried eggs and maple-wood bacon wafted across the room. Someday she would make up for all this with Ann.

Ann lifted the foil from the plate. She set the plate on Jill's desk and told her she loved her. Jill followed the plate down and landed softly in her chair. Ann was soft-spoken, her words full of hope. Another knock on the door came, this time loud enough to snap Ann and Jill out of their locked gaze.

It was the shift sergeant. He told Jill she had a very important call. Jill apologized to Ann and promised she would be home for dinner. Ann lowered her head and turned to leave. Jill jumped up and met her at the door. Ann stopped and turned toward her. They met with a soft embrace as Jill whispered "thank you" in her ear.

Ann smiled. With her head held high, she left Jill to take her call. Jill closed the door.

She returned to her desk, picked up the phone, and pressed the flashing green light to answer the call. The caller introduced himself as John Koch. He told Jill he was pretty sure he recognized the man in the police drawing from the news. He said that he believed he knew where the man worked. John Koch continued talking without Jill saying anything more than her initial "Hello." Koch told Jill he was a long-haul truck driver and every other week or so he picked up a load at a warehouse in Jackson. Said he had seen that fella nearly every time he docked there. Told her he was a quiet fella, kept to himself, worked hard. But that he was sure it was him.

Jill's adrenaline was flowing. A quick glance at the breakfast Ann had prepared for her sent a pang of regret through her guts. She knew it would remain untouched on her desk and would be cold and congealed by the time she returned.

Jill looked at the address and name of the company the truck driver had just given her. She knew the place. It was a small company run by an ex-con. The owner had a solid reputation as a straight shooter and stand-up guy. Nonetheless, she was going to roll over there and get her man.

19

Jill hadn't slept much over the past few days. She was running on all motor, pure drive to catch the bad guy. John Koch had just given her the location of her number one suspect, and a shot of adrenaline. She knew she was close, but she was aware of the danger of rushing. She drew a deep breath, slowly exhaled.

She picked up her phone and called the captain. He said he would have a team ready in two minutes. Eyeing the plate of bacon, she closed her eyes briefly and thought of Ann. Jill stood and grabbed two pieces of the greasy goodness and headed for her car.

Heading out the back door of the post, Jill met with the team of troopers who would back her up as she executed the arrest of her suspect. They huddled under the bright morning sun and quickly reviewed their plan of action. They were ready, confident, and competent.

Jill and her team rolled out of the Jackson State Police post at the corner of Parnall Road and Cooper Street. They were "running cold," no lights or sirens, as they headed south on Cooper Street toward West

Monroe Street. The warehouse their man worked at was at 211 West Monroe, just two miles from their post.

Jill's was the lead car as they pulled into the fenced-in warehouse yard. One car drove around the back. One car blocked the gated entrance from the road. Another blocked the gated exit to the road. The warehouse's large yard would make it easy to see anyone fleeing the building.

With everyone in position, Jill and her backup entered through the employee entrance near the front of the building. The workers all halted immediately; most of them were ex-cons with a healthy respect for law enforcement. The owner of the business walked out of his office to the warehouse floor. He seemed unfazed by the presence of the troopers. The man seemed to know why the cops were there.

Jill ordered the man to halt. She approached him with caution. The warehouse was an open platform with a single office in the front of the structure. If her man was there, he was in that office or in one of the dry vans parked at the docks. She scanned the warehouse floor for her suspect as she showed the owner the artist's rendering. The man told Jill he knew the guy in the drawing and that he had been working there some fifteen years or so. He told Jill he had sent the man home that morning, not enough work to go around, he told her. Jill looked over her shoulder, scanned the warehouse and the amount of apparent work. Nearly every dock had a truck backed into it.

She looked him in the eye. She knew his reputation. She knew he looked out for his workers when they stumbled. He hired ex-cons nobody else would take a risk on and paid them under the table. For her that meant far fewer ex-cons becoming habitual offenders. It gave them a purpose other than dealing drugs or stealing. He often took on more employees than he needed because he couldn't stand to see them turned away when they were making a legitimate effort to be productive, law-abiding citizens. Jill wasn't going to hassle the man.

Instead, she remained calm and asked for the name of her suspect and his address. She asked what he drove, if he drove. She asked if he had any known associates, family, or friends. Jill asked a few more questions about her suspect's past, female relationships, and any odd or particular behaviors that stood out.

The business owner answered all of her questions honestly. He didn't seem to be hiding anything from her. Satisfied with the information, Jill and her team regrouped outside. They would take their man, Max Barnes, at his apartment. She looked at the address: Brookstone Apartments, apartment 3C, Shannon Drive, only a quarter mile away.

20

As Jill and her team broke huddle and went for their respective cars, a call came over the radio: Bill O'Reilly was dead. The stakes had just gone to the next level. Jill's suspect was now wanted for murder one. A new sense of urgency overwhelmed her. She confirmed the information with dispatch, then her team.

She could hold back no longer. She felt like kicking down doors and taking the bad guy down, hard. If her man wasn't at home and she was forced to chase him down, she would make him pay dearly.

She covered the quarter mile to the suspect's location in seconds, slammed on the brakes, and skidded sideways in front of his building. The team followed suit. They took a defensive position behind their cars, ready for action. Jill wanted to take her man down by the book, but if he so much as flinched she was ready to make it rain bullets.

This wasn't a high-crime neighborhood, but they weren't exactly strangers to seeing the five-o rolling through. The people of this neighborhood had seen their share of wannabe gangbangers try to claim their turf as if they were the Gramercy Riffs but end up looking more like the Orphans. Still, the sight of so many cops converging on one apartment with their guns drawn and wearing body armor was drawing attention. Jill needed to get control of the situation quickly.

Before she could move on her guy, she needed to get the gawkers back in their houses. She directed several troopers to clear the area and cover the perimeter. Her heart was pounding. Lyrics to an eighties rock song popped into her head: "Feels like the first time . . ." And it did. It never got easier on her nerves to take a suspect down in this manner. Every encounter with an unknown subject could be the last. Even standard roadside stops for speeding could be fatal for officers not prepared for the worst every time they approached a suspect.

Jill switched on her bullhorn. She called for Max Barnes to come out peacefully. Her instructions were clear and simple. "Come out with your hands up! Kneel on the ground! Place your hands behind your head!"

Through the front window she saw the curtain move. It was a small, nearly indiscernible movement, but she saw it. She knew Max Barnes was there, that he was planning his next move. She felt all her muscles tense like a jungle cat about to pounce on its prey.

Jill gave the signal for her team to hold their positions. She called out to Max Barnes again to surrender. Again, she saw the slightest movement from the curtain. Her stomach growled. Not now, she thought.

Damn it, she wished she'd taken three minutes to eat the breakfast Ann had brought her.

＝

Max Barnes would not go back to prison. He could not go back to prison. Slowly, he pulled the curtain back just a hair. He saw the Michigan State Police, guns drawn, ready to do battle. He was not going out like this, not after everything he had survived. He knew panicking at that moment would not help him.

He stepped back into his small living room and sat down in front of the television. He felt the Ruger tucked into his waistband. Max had been telling himself for years that if it ever came down to this, to losing his freedom, he would not go down without a fight. A war, really. He would make the cops earn their badges. He'd thought it would be easy to just open fire and let the bullets fall where they may. After the first time he was raped in juvenile hall, he had wanted to have the courage to kill the next person who threatened to do him harm of any kind.

But time after time he had succumbed to those who would do him harm. As a free man he had settled into a quasi-comfortable life. He went to work, paid his own way. He had a bed to sleep in, food to eat. He had a private shower and a private commode. Nobody had raped him in a long time. Now he was confronted with the realization that that would all be gone. He knew he needed to stand up and open fire with all guns blazing. Kill or be killed. He had enough ammunition to hold his ground for several hours, maybe even days. He imagined holding out long enough that they would eventually go Waco on him.

Sweat was beading on his brow. He could hear voices all around him. Neighbors shouting at each other about the cops in the street. Mothers shooing their children away from the windows. A news woman on his television.

An alternative solution came to him. A way out. He thought maybe he should just swallow a bullet, end it all on his schedule, on his call. Max slowly pulled the Ruger SR22 from his waistband and put the barrel in his mouth. He pushed the barrel in as far as he could, until it touched the back of his throat and made him gag. His eyes were watering. He could hear a female voice, a cop shouting orders at him. Again he thought of everything he had survived in his pathetic little life and knew that to pull the trigger now would be the ultimate act of betrayal against himself. He hadn't come this far to finish the job for all those miscreants.

21

Jill wished all those damn nosey neighbors would get the hell in their houses and shut their damn doors. Not only were they a distraction to her and her team, but they were putting themselves in harm's way. If this guy Max Barnes didn't surrender peacefully, she and her team were going to open fire as if bullets were free and the governor were handing out awards for most shots fired.

It had been three minutes of silence and stillness. She had seen no additional movement from inside 3C. She wondered if Max Barnes was preparing to barricade himself in and hunker down for battle. Part of her hoped he was; she had a little pent-up energy waiting to be relieved.

The rest of her wished he would just walk out with his hands up and surrender peacefully. She had lost enough of her friends and coworkers to the crazies looking to get their fifteen minutes of fame by killing a cop. She knew she needed to take Max Barnes down before this got out of control.

Jill pulled the trigger on her bullhorn and repeated the order to surrender peacefully. Still no movement from inside. She gave the signal to her team to stand by to make forced entry.

=

Max Barnes removed the Ruger from his mouth and replaced it in his waistband. He heard the stern female voice repeating her orders to surrender peacefully. He looked around his rent-controlled apartment, his little corner in the projects. The outcome of this situation did not look good. He thought his odds were rather bleak.

Outside his apartment in the ghetto were at least a dozen cops waiting to either arrest him or kill him. Even so, he found himself looking at the news woman on his tiny television and wondered what made people want to sit in that box and read the sensationalized headlines of murder, rape, and corruption every day. What had happened to Bill O'Reilly that compelled him to go into the news business? And why did he even care about Bill O'Reilly?

Max drew a breath, leaned his head back, and closed his eyes. For a moment he felt as if he were in a vacuum, a void. It was black, and silent, and still. He could no longer feel the sweat on his brow or the clamminess of his palms. He could not feel his heart beating, or his lungs expanding and contracting. There were no cops outside. There was no news lady reading the headlines. He was at total peace when a stun grenade shattered his front window and a battering ram obliterated his front door. The bright flash blinded him as if he had looked directly at the sun. His ears felt as if they were bleeding. The side of his face nearest the window stung as if he'd just been slapped by his mother for angering his father.

A moment after experiencing what Max could only imagine as serenity, he was face down on his musty carpet, a knee on his neck and several more on his back as his arms were twisted behind him. He felt the cold steel of handcuffs being clamped around his wrists.

22

The takedown was swift, aggressive, and well organized. Jill had public enemy number one under her boot. She was a little surprised—and relieved—when he did not resist. He didn't surrender peacefully like she had hoped, but at least he did not come out all guns blazing.

And from what Jill and her team found inside the tiny apartment, he could have put up one serious fight. There were multiple guns and hundreds of rounds of ammunition within spitting distance of where they'd taken their man down, including a fully loaded Ruger SR22 in his waistband, a pistol that fired .22 long rifle bullets.

When the smoke settled and Max Barnes had been cuffed and hauled out of the apartment, Jill saw the newspaper clippings and pictures of Bill O'Reilly on the walls. All of the pictures had a prohibition sign—a red circle with a slash—drawn on them in red marker.

The scene was clear to Jill; she had caught a killer, a psychopath. Max Barnes had obviously been stalking

Bill O'Reilly for some time, his hatred fermenting, plotting an assassination.

Jill walked through the killer's den. The tiny apartment had little furniture: a ragged lounge chair, a small television atop an end table, and, in the walk-in-closet-sized bedroom, a single bed and a three-drawer dresser. The kitchenette was sparse: an ancient stove-top coffee percolator, a few dirty dishes in the sink. The refrigerator was full of cheap sandwich meats and generic diet cola. Scattered throughout both rooms were stacks of newspapers and tabloid magazines. Aside from the relatively modern television, the place could have been furnished by Sanford and Son.

Jill came back to the living room wall and stared at the pictures and newspaper clippings of O'Reilly. She was amazed and horrified by the level of hatred Max Barnes harbored for Bill O'Reilly. She wondered what Max Barnes had seen Bill O'Reilly do, or what he had heard Bill O'Reilly say, to spark such hatred.

=

A small army of Michigan State Troopers led Max out of his home. Outside in the bright morning sun, dozens of voyeurs watched intently as Max was placed in the back of a squad car. He was still seeing bright spots in his eyes, and his ears were still ringing from the stun grenade. Max sat with his head up, watching the action, feeling removed from it as if he were watching it on television. He could not wrap his mind around what was happening to him. He just could not believe it. As the car sped away, tires squealing, radio crackling, he cursed himself for not opening fire on the cops and taking a stand.

Max didn't know what was going to happen to him, but he was sure it would not be anything good. That was just how things worked out for him.

23

Late on the evening of 12 August 2014, Jill and Ann sat on the couch with the lights off watching *The Daily Show with Jon Stewart*. Jon was doing a special piece on Bill O'Reilly, a sort of tribute; Jill thought it was heartfelt and sincere. She suspected Jon and Bill were closer friends than their on-air personas would allow them to show. Jill never pretended to understand either of those particular entertainers or celebrities in general, but intuition told her that those men had appreciated each other.

It had been a long day, a long weekend. She had been operating on very little sleep and even less food. She'd missed Ann while she worked on the O'Reilly case and meant to make up for lost time. But even though Max Barnes was behind bars, her case was not closed.

As she sat watching, an arm around Ann holding her close, she ran through the case in her mind. She was so tired. The evidence was all mixed up in her head. Her eyelids drooped closed. She heard, "And now, ladies and gentlemen, here it is, your moment of Zen."

"Maxie. Maxie. It's getting late now." Jill felt a tap on her shoulder, the voice barely a whisper. She had gone to bed early in anticipation of going fishing with her father. Few things were better than waking up early to go fishing with her father. But she was so tired; the night had passed so quickly. She felt as if she had just put her head on her pillow.

"Maxie, come on now. We want to get to the fishing hole before sunup." Jill could smell fresh-cut hay and coffee. She moaned and tried to open her eyes, but her eyelids were too heavy.

"Maxie, you feeling OK? Is something the matter?" Jill felt a light shake of her shoulder. She tried to roll onto her back. She wanted to look at her father and tell him she was OK. She moaned softly instead.

"Sometimes you have to just force yourself to push through whatever problem stands in front of you, Maxie." Jill wanted to tell her father she was just tired, that she just needed ten more minutes of sleep and she would get up.

"I miss you, Maxie, very much. Not a day goes by that I don't think about you." Jill's chest got tight. She could feel the tears welling.

"I'm sorry I had to leave you and your mother. I wish I could have stayed." Jill wanted to tell her father that she missed him too, but she couldn't find her voice.

"Maxie, I love you." Jill's throat tightened as she tried to tell her father how much she loved him. No matter how hard she tried, she couldn't get the words to come out.

Jill was crying; the scent of her father had vanished.

When Jill opened her eyes, the television had been switched off, the room was pitch-dark, and she could feel Ann's shallow breaths of deep sleep against her shoulder. She touched her cheek and felt the warm tears from her dream. She looked at the screen on her mobile and saw it was after 3 a.m. So much for making up for lost time with Ann. She needed to get to her office; she needed to interview Max Barnes.

24

As the sun rose on 13 August, Jill wanted nothing more than to make Ann breakfast in bed, then spend the rest of the day in bed with her. What she did was not that. She slipped out the back door and got in her car. She had a long day ahead of her, and she needed to get an early start.

Jill went to her office to review the evidence again. It still did not add up for her that Max Barnes was the killer.

She pulled up his personal file, hoping for some insight. He had spent time in juvenile hall for assault and battery against a schoolmate, a pretty violent attack, according to the report. There were no school records after that year, which led Jill to assume he had run away from home and school; his parents both had petty rap sheets a mile long, so no surprise there. When he was just seventeen, he had been convicted of killing a junkie and sent to the penitentiary. He'd served fifteen years inside Jacktown, racking up several misconducts and a few stints in the infirmary. He was paroled in 1987 and had basically remained under the radar since.

From the look of his apartment, Max Barnes spent all of his leisure time watching television and stalking Bill O'Reilly. But why Bill O'Reilly? She was going to the jail to interview him.

Jill sat in her car for a moment before going into the jail. Her job—her life, really—was all about catching the bad guys. Once she'd tracked them down and arrested them, her job was done for the most part. Sometimes she testified at trial when the defendant refused to cop to a plea deal, and she even went to the jail on occasion to interview suspects when she had to. But she didn't enjoy those parts of the job the way she did chasing the bad guys. Going to the jail was one of the hardest parts of the job for Jill; for one thing, she didn't like the smell, a cross between a ripe dog kennel and a hospital waiting room. The inmates were only issued fresh blues once per week, and the cleaning was done by inmates who had "earned" trustee status. Many of the inmates already had poor hygiene habits before they came in, but they seemed to care even less once they became part of the system.

The thing that Jill really disliked about going into the jail to interview a suspect, though, was the feeling of doubt that sometimes crept up on her. Inside the concrete and steel, with pale gray floors and walls, and the too-bright fluorescent lights, Jill imagined some of these guys to be like wild animals in a zoo: maybe not well mannered, or exactly intelligent, but also not guilty of anything other than circumstance. She thought Max Barnes might fit that category.

Jill shook her head as if erasing a macabre scene from an Etch-a-Sketch. She took a deep breath and headed for the door.

She signed in, went through the mandatory pat-down, and walked through the metal detector. It frustrated her that enough cops had been busted smuggling in dope and other contraband that even the highest-ranking cops with the cleanest records were treated like any other visitor.

Even in the early morning, the county jail was not a quiet place. The thick concrete walls and floors sent every sound wave ricocheting back and forth down the halls, voices—talking and shouting—and mop buckets full of dirty water squeaking and clanging along the corridors. The public-address system seemed more like a form of torture than communication as it crackled and hissed between continuous interruptions from the command center blasting announcements nobody could understand.

Jill waited in the command center while Barnes was escorted from his cell in ad-seg to an eight-by-eight interrogation room. Even though to Jill cops and corrections officers were all on the same team, she often felt like an outsider encroaching on the COs' turf. They seemed to her to just go through the motions, making no effort to expedite the process or assist beyond just doing the job. She knew they all had their own jobs to do, but after forty-five minutes of waiting she was starting to get pissed. Just as she was clearing her throat to let the command control officer know she was growing impatient, the call came over the radio that she was cleared to come back.

=

Max Barnes lay on his bunk staring at the dirty gray concrete ceiling; he had been here before, but this time felt different. The way the guards walked by his cell, the look in their eyes, scared him. He was old and tired. He had been beaten down time and time again, somehow managing to get back on his feet, but he could never get ahead. But now—now he knew his number was up, his ticket had been punched. He closed his eyes, hoping to sleep a little, or with any luck sleep forever.

Unfortunately for Max, he would get no rest this morning, as the heavy steel door closing off ad-seg clanked open and a guard stopped in front of his cell. The CO told Max he had a visitor. Max had no family and no friends. He had not been assigned legal representation by the court yet; he wasn't scheduled to see the judge for his arraignment until the following day. Max didn't say anything because it would not have mattered; inside these walls, you did what you were told when you were told to do it.

Max was shackled, his ankles together and his wrists together and a long chain connecting the two—an inmate's version of being hobbled. It didn't bother Max to have his wrists chained to his ankles, not really. But he never got used to walking with the leg irons on. The chain was just long enough to walk heel to toe, and that short of a step was just not natural, and more than a little humiliating.

Nonetheless, Max hobbled on, a half step ahead of the guard. Max would not have tried to fight his way out of jail at the peak of his fitness; he certainly was not going to try in his current decrepit state.

He was led to a small room with formed concrete benches along two opposing walls. There was no table, no chairs, only a thick steel ring jutting out of one wall and another jutting out of the base of the bench below. Max was led in, his wrist irons chained to the top ring, his leg irons chained to the bottom. For a fleeting moment, being chained so heavily made him feel crazy strong, the way he imagined a steroid freak felt after juicing. After the moment passed, he laughed a little at himself for having such an absurd thought. He looked at his weak wrists and chicken legs. Pathetic.

There was no way to be comfortable on the concrete bench, in chains, wearing an oversized blue jumpsuit and hard rubber flip flops. So he sat with his shoulders hunched inward, his elbows on his thighs, and his ankles together and waited for his mystery visitor.

Max had no idea how long he'd been waiting in the tiny room when he heard the key turning the lock in the plate-steel door.

25

The guard pulled open the vault-like door and stepped aside for Jill to enter to the room. The harsh fluorescent light tucked securely behind the mesh-steel grate was flickering sporadically, giving her a headache as she crossed the threshold into the room.

She eyed Max as she sat down across from him. He was smaller than she remembered from his arrest, older too. The gray stubble on his chin looked coarse like steel bristles on a wire brush. His skin was tight and weathered. His fingers were gnarled and his fingernails dirty. He had thick calluses on his bony hands.

Jill wanted to know about Max and how he'd come to hate Bill O'Reilly and why he'd been at the Michigan Theatre the night O'Reilly was shot in the face. She looked at Max a moment longer, searching for something in his eyes, maybe even hoping she would find something in there worth saving.

There was little good she could see in there. He sat motionless while she pulled a digital recorder from her breast pocket and turned it on. She said, "Hi, Max, I'm Inspector Jill Brown with the Michigan State Police, and I'm here to ask you some questions. You are not obligated to answer any questions, or even to say anything without an attorney present. It's up to you. This isn't a game to me. And I'm sure this doesn't feel like a game to you. What do you say; do you want to talk?"

Max remained silent. She looked him in the eye as he sat up a little straighter on the cold bench, his chains clinking softly.

=

Max didn't trust people in general or cops in particular. They were all liars. None of them cared, not really. But there was something different about this cop that put Max a little at ease. It was something in the way she looked at him. She didn't look at him like the others did, the way they mean-mugged him through the bars. She had kindness in her dark brown eyes, warmth and compassion. Max imagined she probably brought home stray animals to nurse them back to health before finding forever homes for them.

She didn't seem intimidated by him, or afraid. Not that he thought he was an intimidating person or someone who instilled fear in the hearts of men, or women. But it was the *way* she wasn't intimidated or afraid that struck him. She had a confidence that was easily perceived.

Max looked up at the inspector when she had finished and said, "Nobody cares about what I've done, where I've been, what I've seen. Nobody ever cared. What difference does it make to you?"

He watched as she leaned a little forward and rested her elbows on her knees, not like she was trying to invade his personal space but more like she was closing a personal gap between them, making the conversation intimate rather than intimidating.

Before she could answer, he added, "And I don't need a lawyer in here if I decide to talk you. There is not a thing you can do to me that has not been done before." He decided if she wanted to hear his life story, to know him, then he would tell her.

26

Jill said, "Max, a man is dead, a very popular celebrity whose murder is drawing a lot of attention. You are charged with his murder. Do you understand that? The seriousness of the charge? If this was premeditated—and by all accounts that is the one thing that is certain—you're facing the death penalty. Doesn't that worry you at all?"

Max held her gaze. He wondered what worried her at night. He said, "No. I didn't kill Bill O'Reilly."

It was Jill's turn to hold his gaze. She could count on one hand the number of suspects who admitted to the crime they had been booked on. It didn't matter how petty or how serious the charge—bad guys rarely admitted responsibility. But when Max Barnes looked at her with his dark eyes and said he hadn't killed Bill O'Reilly, it sounded like a recited fact. Like there was no doubt that that was the only answer he could have given her. She had met plenty of suspects who beat the polygraph test only to be found guilty later with concrete evidence such as DNA, fingerprints, or video surveillance. Even then most of them never admitted guilt.

Max added, "I didn't like the guy, and I thought about killing him. I even went to the theater with the intent to kill him. But I didn't. I'm not the guy."

Jill had read Max's file; she knew he was capable of murder, but she also knew that what made it into a suspect's file was only one side of the story. She wanted to hear his side. She let his last statement hang in the air for a few moments. She wanted to start at the beginning, with his parents. She took a short silent breath, looked him squarely in the eye, and said, "Max, when was the last time you saw your parents?"

Max's jaw tightened reflexively. He had no good memories of his parents and hadn't expected the cop to go there. He said, "If you want to talk about my parents, then maybe we should end this conversation right now."

Jill didn't want to lose him already, but she wanted to know what his parents were like. She knew the relationship between parent and child was the foundation for a person's life. It was where they developed their social skills and ethics. It was their imprint for how to treat others and what treatment to expect from others. Jill pressed on. "Max, listen, I have your file. It feels like there is a lot missing. All I'm asking from you is to fill in the gaps. What happened before Freddy Green? What happened between juvenile hall and prison? What happened between prison and Bill O'Reilly? I want to know about your parents. Tell me about them."

The muscles in Max's jaw relaxed a little. He exhaled loudly through his nose. Max said, "You want to know about my parents? Pssht! Wild animals have more love and respect for their offspring.

"When I was just about five years old, my father came home late one night. Nothing new there, he came home late a lot. He was drunk. One of those guys who walked around with a pint of whiskey in his back pocket and drank straight from the bottle. I was in my bedroom, not really sleeping but wishing I was. Mother was in the kitchen playing solitaire and drinking a glass of beer. She used to shake salt into her glass of beer. I can still see the millions of bubbles racing to the top of the glass." Max grunted in disgust.

"I'm in bed. It's real dark. I hear the front door slam. Then my father is saying something; it sounds like his teeth are clenched. When he was mad he always talked through clenched teeth. Then I heard chairs sliding across the kitchen floor. I heard my mother suck in a sharp breath and then the sound of breaking glass. I tried to cover my ears, but it didn't stop the sound of him smacking her. She screamed and he hit her harder. I could hear the table being pushed around.

"By then I was crying. I pressed my hands to my eyes to try and block the tears. The fighting went on for another minute or two. I heard my father grinding out a few more insults, and then he started laughing. My mother was crying. She sounded like a wounded animal whimpering.

"I thought it was over and that maybe he would leave again. But he didn't. I heard his heavy footsteps coming toward my room. I fought back the tears as hard as I could. He stopped just outside my door. I took a deep breath and tried to hold it until he left, but he swung open my door. I peeked through my fingers and saw his black figure against the hallway light. He was breathing heavily. There was a glint barely visible just above his belt.

"He just stood there for a minute. He was looking right into my eyes through the tiny cracks between my fingers. It felt like he was looking inside of me. I could swear he was smiling. That only scared me more."

Jill felt the hair on her arms prickling.

"He said, 'Hey, boy!' and I tried to act like I didn't hear him, but he said it again. I put my hands down just a little and looked at him. He said, 'I knew you was awake. Let's play a game.' My father never played games. I was scared. Even then, at five years old, I knew it was going to be bad.

"He walked over and sat on the bed next to me and pulled me up in to a sitting position. I could see clearly then that the glint had been a pistol tucked into his waistband. His eyes were wild, flicking left and right. His breath was hot and smelled like booze. He said, 'You cryin', boy? Cryin' is for babies and little girls.' It took everything I had not to cry.

"I just sat there looking at his face, trying not to look at the gun. I'd never seen him with a gun before. I wasn't sure how long he'd had it. It didn't really matter; he had it that night. I must have glanced at the gun, because he looked from my face to the gun real quick, then laughed and pulled it out. My lips were trembling.

"The light from the hallway shone on him like a spotlight on a magician surrounded by darkness. He held the gun in front of him. It was a revolver. He flicked it open and dumped all the bullets into his hand. I watched his hands closely as he put one bullet back in, spun the cylinder, then snapped his wrist to close it.

"For a few seconds he just looked at the gun, smiling. Then he put the barrel to my forehead and said, 'Boys don't cry, boy,' pulled the hammer back, then yelled, 'Bang!'

"I pissed myself right then. He just started howling. I was scared to death. He stood up, slapped me across the back of the head, and said, 'Don't be such a girl.'"

Jill realized she'd slid to the edge of the concrete bench and slowly pushed herself back to the wall.

"There I was, soaked in piss, scared outta my mind but glad he was leaving. I heard his footsteps all the way to the door, then I heard the door slam. I was still sitting up on the edge of my bed in the dark when I heard my mother rustling in the kitchen. I heard cabinet doors opening and closing and chairs being dragged across the floor. Then I heard her coming toward my room; she was crying but it didn't sound the same as earlier. She was breathing harder and sucking air between her trembling lips."

Jill hoped the story wouldn't get any worse. But she sensed it was just the beginning.

"She marched straight into my room. I could see she was holding a clothes hanger. At that moment she looked scarier than my father. Unlike my father though, she got right to the point and started whipping me with the hanger. Also unlike my father she didn't say a word;

she just whipped and whipped until her arms were too tired to whip anymore."

Pity was the only thing Jill felt at that moment.

"After she exhausted herself whipping me, she collapsed on the bed next to me and sobbed into my blanket. My arms and back were covered in bloody welts. And then the worst thing happened."

No, it can't get worse, Jill thought.

"She wrapped her arms around me and pulled me in close to her, so close she was hurting me. She started kissing my shoulders. She was babbling through tears and snot about how much she loved me and how sorry she was. And kept on until she finally fell asleep right there in my bed, still holding me in a death grip. I'm not sure how much longer I stayed awake. In the morning she was gone. Gone out of my bed, gone out of the house. When she showed up a week later, she acted like nothing ever happened.

"Does that paint a clear enough picture of my parents?"

As bad as that had been to hear, Jill knew there was more. She had to keep it together without showing too much emotion. Too much emotion in this situation could lead a suspect to feel like he had power over the interrogator. She said, "Max, what really happened with Freddy Green? The file says you kicked in his teeth and it took several male teachers to pull you off of him?"

27

Max had never seen this file she kept bringing up, but it sounded like it didn't have any of the facts right. He said, "Freddy Green? Yeah, I kicked his teeth in, all right."

Max went on and told Jill about Freddy the bully. He told Jill about all the bullying from all the kids; even girls had picked on him. He told her how even his teachers seemed to be in on the game. He told how it was him against the world at twelve.

Jill had heard plenty of stories about victims of bullying who got revenge. She had seen the effects of bullying. She was aware of the statistics on how victims of bullying became domestic abusers, rapists, and murderers. But how had Max ended up spending a year in juvenile hall for defending himself against a known bully?

She asked, "You sustained obvious injuries that day, serious ones? But you were seen as the aggressor? What happened?"

Max had relived that day too many times already. At his age he felt foolish trying to justify what he'd done to Fat Freddy Green. But he saw sincerity in the inspector's eyes. He said, "I didn't have to go to juvenile hall for what happened. I think my parents saw my getting arrested as a way to get a break from me.

"The juvenile authorities came for me at the jail because my parents refused to come down and sign for me. That's all they had to do: come to the jail and sign a piece of paper, and I could have gone home. But I wasn't worth even that little bit of effort to them.

"Not that home was necessarily a better place to be, but it was home. I was familiar with it even if it was a living hell. Being locked away like an animal at twelve and having your parents abandon you can really mess with your head.

"They wouldn't have even showed up at my hearing if the judge had not subpoenaed them. They were there, and I could tell that made them mad. It was just one more way I screwed them.

"The hearing didn't take long. The judge read the file, the prosecutor recommended a year in juvenile hall, and my court-appointed attorney agreed to it. The judge asked my parents if they had anything to say about it. My father looked over at me and crunched up his face and told the judge that whatever time he gave me wouldn't be enough to straighten me out. My mother remained silent. She wouldn't even look at me.

"I thought about begging my parents not to let them take me but decided that whatever time away from them would be a break for me too.

"After the judge sentenced me to a year in juvenile hall, he asked my parents if they wanted a minute alone with me to say goodbye. They just grunted at him and shook their heads in disgust. And that was it."

Jill was shocked by the callousness of Max's parents. She thought about her parents, about her dad and how much he had loved her. The word *pity* kept running through her mind. She asked, "What happened after the year?"

Max hadn't talked this much in his whole life, but he felt like he was in too deep to stop now. He said, "I'm not sure why, but my mother came to pick me up the day I was released. She didn't look well. It was the first time I felt sorry for her. She brought up my father and told me that he couldn't wait to see me. I knew she was lying. By the time we got to the car, I was trying to figure out how to get away. I didn't want to go home; I couldn't go back. I jumped out of the car and ran until I couldn't run anymore.

"I knew she would pay for letting me run away, but I didn't care anymore. She was just as evil as him, and I just wanted out."

Jill was looking at his face so intently that she hadn't realized he'd stopped talking. There was an empty moment before he added, "I never saw them again. I can only hope they died slow, painful deaths."

28

Few stories had horrified Jill more than Max's. But she didn't want to hear any more about Max's childhood or his parents. She got it; they were bad people and they'd probably paid for it. She hoped they'd paid for it. She wanted to know why he'd gone to the theater to kill Bill O'Reilly.

She said, "Max, you were released from prison in 1987 after fifteen years down. You basically disappeared in plain view. No arrests, no traffic violations, no collections, no taxes, no hospitalizations, nothing. On paper it appears that you dropped out of the race. For fifteen years you blend in, lay low. You go to work, you go home. Then, seemingly out of nowhere, you end up at the Michigan Theatre with a gun and Bill O'Reilly ends up dead from a bullet to the face. It doesn't make sense."

Max straightened up, leaned back against the unforgiving concrete wall, and said, "I told you, I didn't kill Bill O'Reilly. I'm not saying he didn't deserve to die; he did. But I didn't kill him."

Jill said, "What's with the all the pictures and clippings about O'Reilly? What did you have against him? Hate doesn't seem like a strong enough word to describe the scene in your apartment."

Max seemed to be searching for the right words to answer her. Jill wondered whether even he knew why he'd gone there that night. Maybe it was a momentary lapse of reason. Maybe he was afflicted with temporary insanity. Hell, maybe he was actually insane. He sure had good enough reason to be. In the silence of the moment, Jill started thinking that was the answer: he was insane.

Then Max spoke. "Sitting here now, talking to you about all this, about my parents, my life . . . I'm not so sure about things. It seems like just the other day I was a small boy hiding in my closet, scared to death of my parents, the people who were supposed to love me and protect me. Even then I knew that wasn't how it should have been. I knew they were evil. Then one day I realized I was an old man, sitting in a ragged old chair watching a busted-up old TV.

"I never had a childhood, no friends on the playground, no Saturday afternoon baseball games, no sleepovers. I never felt the touch of a woman, never had anyone tell me they loved me. I've been alone my whole life, see. Never trusted anyone, no reason to."

Jill interrupted him. "Max, what did you have against O'Reilly?"

"What did I have against him? I trusted him. He made me believe in him."

"Wait. You trusted him, so you wanted him dead?"

"No. At first I trusted him, when I started watching him on TV. My whole life people had been lying to me.

I couldn't trust anyone. Then I saw him on TV talking about how a guy can't trust anyone anymore because so few people have integrity. He said he was tired of crooked politicians getting away with murder and how the media distorts the facts and the truth and how people just don't take responsibility for their actions anymore. All that talk, I felt all the same things. I felt like he understood me. So I kept on watching him. Every night I came home and watched the news and heard all the BS, and then I would turn on his show and hear the truth. He cut right to the chase. He didn't let anyone off with fluff questions and didn't let anyone pass a lie on him. He was quick to stomp out people who came on his show to promote a lie. I trusted him to tell me the truth."

Jill was perplexed. She hadn't been expecting Max to tell her how much he trusted the guy he was accused of killing. She said, "Max, listen, this doesn't add up. You say in the beginning you trusted him? So what happened to make you go from trusting him to wanting to kill him?"

"Simple. He was a liar just like all the rest. No. He was worse. He went on TV every night and condemned everyone else for lying and cheating and being corrupt. He was the worst liar of them all. When I realized I had been fooled again, I got mad. I thought someone oughta do something about the guy. Make a point. Not just write the guy a letter telling him he was a liar; he already knew that. I wanted to send a message to everyone on TV like him.

"I figured I wasn't getting any younger, my health was getting worse every day, and I didn't really have anything to lose. So I started thinking of how I could kill the guy. But it didn't take long to figure out he was too far away. I couldn't get to New York so I shelved the idea. I kept watching his show and keeping track of all the lies he told. I started collecting pictures of him and newspaper stories. For a while I figured he was just another person I wanted dead but couldn't do anything about. Then he announced he was coming to Jackson to do his show. I hadn't been that excited about anything my whole life. He was coming to my hometown, and I decided I would take action. I bought myself a ticket to the show and started working on a plan."

"Max, where did you get the guns and ammunition? You had enough firepower to wage a small war."

"That was the easy part. I picked 'em up at yard sales and what not. They all came with ammo. Nobody ever asked me what I wanted 'em for. After I bought the first one and found out how easy it was, I bought a few more, you know, just in case."

Jill's head was spinning. She hated how easy it was for criminals to buy guns and ammunition. This guy had been convicted of a violent assault as a juvenile and murder as an adult and was able to go to a neighborhood yard sale and buy guns like he was buying yard tools. She hated all the gun laws that just made it harder for law-abiding citizens to buy guns but did nothing to prevent or even slow down gun violence. Sometimes she hated herself for not having a better solution to the problem.

She asked "What happened at the theater?"

Max said, "I went with the intention of killing him, or least trying to. After I got there, I got real nervous about doing it. I thought, *What the hell am I doing here?* Then, bam! The guy gets shot in the face and the whole place goes crazy. It was like a dream. I couldn't believe what had happened. I mean, there I was with my hand on my gun thinking about what it would feel like to pull the trigger, and someone did. I got the hell outta there."

"How did you drop your gun, Max?"

"I don't know. I guess from all the pushing and shoving it fell out of my waistband."

"And that's when you met Jeannie Redmont? The woman who saw you picking the gun up from the floor?"

"Yeah, she was real scared. I don't blame her. It was a pretty crazy scene."

"So you got out of the theater before the cops came?"

"Yeah, I made it out just as they were pulling up. I ducked around the corner and walked home. For the next few days I laid low. And well, you know the rest."

She didn't know the rest. But she'd gotten what she wanted from him. She had heard enough. She stood and called for the guard to open the door. Max remained seated. He just watched her walk out the door without saying another word.

29

Jill walked out of the jailhouse and into the blinding sunlight. The battery indicator on her digital recorder was flashing, a poignant reminder of her own exhaustion. Her head was spinning from the interview with Max Barnes. She felt a lot of things about him, none of them good, but she didn't believe he was the killer.

He'd answered her questions candidly, she was sure.

When she opened the car door, a wave of heat rolled out, nearly taking her breath away. She hesitated just a moment before sliding in and turning the ignition key. She turned the AC knob to high. Max's tragic story made her think of her own childhood and how great her parents had been. She couldn't imagine being in Max's place.

She made a mental note to make a trip to her mother's place one day next weekend. Her mother had never remarried. She'd told Jill a few years after her father's death that he was the only man she could ever love, that once he was gone that that part of her—the part that makes a woman desire a man—was gone too.

Twenty minutes had passed by in the blink of eye. Jill realized she was crying, softly, tears running in a steady stream down her cheeks. She knew it was partly because of Max's story, partly because she missed her parents, and partly because she was just too damned tired.

She finally pulled the shifter into reverse and backed out of the parking space. She was going home to see Ann before she thought of any more questions for Max.

30

I t was early morning on 14 August, the sun just falling off the other side of Earth. Jill lay awake staring into the darkness. She had tossed and turned through the night, restless and agitated. The events of the week had taken a tremendous toll on her psyche. She had been a cop a long time, and before this week the word "retire" had been just a word her coworkers used in jokes after they had a bad day; retiring was not something she'd ever considered.

Over her career Jill had seen just about every bad thing one person could do to another. In college she'd studied criminal behavior, psychology, and the justice system. Back then, in the beginning, she thought it all made perfect sense. Every type of behavior had been put into a neat little category and given a fancy name, and Jill and all her classmates studied them and memorized them and scored high marks on all their exams. The part about living with your own personal catalog of criminals, victims, and behaviors was never mentioned in class. Sure, there were plenty of horror stories told nights at the bar over endless pitchers of beer and rows of empty shot glasses, but nothing was put in perspective; it all felt glorified.

Jill's father had been killed while on duty; his death was the deciding factor in her becoming a cop. She'd thought she wanted to do it to continue his legacy, to prove his life had meant something. But staring into the darkness, Ann nestled tightly against her, she couldn't think of a reason to continue doing the job.

Her mother had lost her husband, the only man she had ever been with, to the job and had paid with a lifetime of heartache and loneliness. Jill knew she had been more than lucky on the job. She had taken too many unnecessary risks and managed to come out alive.

She knew it wasn't just her father's death or Max's life that was making her think it was time to get out of the game; maybe she couldn't put a name on it or find it in her textbooks, but she knew what she felt.

Ann stirred next to her, stretched her arms over her head, and yawned. Jill thought at that moment if she had to put a name on it, that name would be Ann.

Ann curled up in Jill's arms and fell back asleep. Jill held her tight, their breathing in sync, and closed her eyes.

The phone next to the bed rang, and Jill blinked open her eyes, realizing she had finally drifted off to much-needed sleep. It rang again and she looked over at the clock next to it. In the blink of an eye, it was 10 a.m. She was supposed to be in her office working on the Barnes/O'Reilly case. The phone rang a third time, and she reached over and answered it. When she put the phone to her ear, she heard the captain's voice.

At first she thought he was scolding her for not showing up. But he wasn't. He said he was calling with news about Max Barnes; he had been found dead in his cell early that morning. Jill was shocked. She asked how that could happen in ad-seg under watch, but even as she asked the question she knew the answer wouldn't change a thing. The captain told her that Barnes had been found lying next to the toilet, out of view of the surveillance camera. He said Barnes apparently died of asphyxiation. He had wads of wet toilet paper jammed in his throat.

Jill replaced the phone receiver and laid her head back on the pillow.

31

It took several minutes for the news of Max Barnes's death to sink in for Jill. Suicide? She supposed it was possible, but she hadn't gotten the feeling he was suicidal. He could have taken his life any time before his arrest. She had seen more than one suspect eat a bullet after being surrounded by police. Max could have put his gun in his mouth and done the same; he'd had plenty of warning he was going down. But he hadn't. He'd let police take him down without firing a single shot.

And suicide by asphyxiation? Max had suffered many terrible events in his life, but he didn't seem like the kind of guy—desperate and out of touch with reality—who could shove wads of wet toilet paper down his throat until he choked to death. He was a survivor if nothing else.

Max had survived some of the most horrendous things a person could imagine. Had his arrest been the final straw for him? Was the prospect of another trial too much? The idea of spending the rest of his life in prison?

Jill wanted to see the body. She wanted to talk to the guard who'd been on duty and see his log entries, and if everything went really well maybe she could get a look at the security footage. There were so many questions that needed to be answered.

Leaning on one elbow, Jill realized Ann was not in bed with her. She heard the clanking of a skillet on the stove and was suddenly aware of the comforting smell of frying maple-wood bacon wafting in. Her stomach growled. She slipped on her robe and followed the delicious smells to the kitchen.

She met Ann in the kitchen, thanked her for making such a wonderful brunch, then apologized for having to eat on the run as she folded two pieces of bacon and one fried egg in a pancake—sans syrup—and headed for the shower.

With her mind cleared from the hot shower and her stomach settled from the quick breakfast, Jill was ready to get some answers.

Ann walked her to the door. On her way out, Jill told Ann she had something she wanted to talk with her about when she got home. Some good news for a change, she said. Jill sat in her car looking at Ann for a moment before starting the engine and driving away.

Jill went to the jail and signed in. She met with the shift supervisor and asked to see the inmate count log from the night shift. The supervisor gave Jill a long cold stare. Jill continued and asked the name of the night shift guard. The supervisor continued staring, his expression unchanged. Cops didn't question cops. That was the fastest way to finding yourself out of the loop, permanently. He told her that would not be possible because the log had already been turned over as evidence. He told her not to worry about the guard's name or anything else regarding the dead inmate.

Something told Jill there was more to the story than met the eye, but she knew better than to push the issue. The supervisor had been firm in his answer to her request, and she saw in his eyes that he wasn't going to budge. She didn't feel like burning any bridges on her way out, so she thanked the shift supervisor and headed back to her office.

Noon was quickly approaching as Jill picked up her phone and called the captain. She cut straight to the matter at hand and asked him why she was being blocked from looking into Barnes's death. The captain told her to let it go, that the sheriff was looking into the matter and would handle his people.

The captain and Jill went back a long way, to her rookie year when he was already a seasoned sergeant, so he offered a little information to hopefully curb her interest. Barnes had been observed sleeping peacefully at the 5 a.m. count, but during the 6 a.m. count at shift change he was found lying next to the toilet, dead. Even in administrative segregation, Michigan state law prohibited cameras from viewing the toilet area. A review of the security footage revealed a four-minute gap in the recording from 5:36 a.m. to 5:40 a.m. The gap was attributed to an undetected power surge in the modem controlling all of the cameras in ad-seg. Barnes was visible in the footage prior to the surge but never came back in the frame after the modem reset. The officer on duty assumed Barnes was "on the can."

He reminded her that her victim was Bill O'Reilly and that their number one suspect was now dead. He recommended taking the rest of the day off.

Inmate deaths weren't unheard of in the jail, but they weren't commonplace either, and every death, even the ones that appeared to be obvious suicides, was investigated. The sheriff was obligated to look into Barnes' death; if he found negligence on the part of his people, he would handle it internally, and if he found evidence of criminal activity, he would turn it over to the DA.

By the end of the day, Jill received word that the case had been officially closed. Barnes was the guy, and he was dead. The coroner had confirmed that the cause of death was suicide by asphyxiation. There were no signs of a struggle in the cell, no marks on the body, and no witnesses to the death. The power surge had been confirmed by the IT department. The sheriff had concluded that his staff had followed protocol and therefore no further investigation was warranted.

Jill didn't argue with the captain; there was no point. It was out of her hands. She sat in her chair for a few minutes and thought how quickly the case had run its course. Things moved very quickly in real life. She wished there were a Hollywood director standing beside her, yelling, "Cut, cut, let's do it again, people, we have to get it right!"

Jane White lives in Storrs, Connecticut with her wife Alicia and their Doberman Pinchers Bert and Ernie. She is a registered Democrat and professed Progressive Liberal. By day Jane creates unique metal sculptures using welding, forging, and blacksmithing. By night she writes fiction.

CPSIA information can be obtained
at www.ICGtesting.com
Printed in the USA
BVOW06s1825250917
495858BV00017B/141/P